ENDED?

MODERN LOVE BOOK 2

KILBY BLADES

For the fandom.

For permission requests and other inquiries, reach Kilby at kilby@kilbyblades.com.

Amazon Print ISBN: 978-1-954653-06-1

PART 1
WALKING ON SUNSHINE

1 WALKING ON SUNSHINE

I used to think maybe you loved me, now I know
    that it's true.
And I don't want to spend my whole life
just a-waiting for you.
Now I don't want you back for the weekend,
not back for a day.
I said baby I just want you back,
and I want you to stay.
-Katrina and the Waves, Walking on
Sunshine

JAGGER (LATE AUGUST)

"This is just wrong."

Declan's proclamation was spoken from the back seat of my car, his bass low, his words slow, and his tone grim. A glance in my rearview mirror caught the scowl on his face as he glared out the window toward the quad. He looked every bit as put-out as he had ten minutes before, when I'd picked him up from his house.

"I mean...is this even legal?" he groused. "Technically, it's still summer vacation. Why should a college counselor have the right to make us come to school? Miss Morales ought to be reported to the authorities. This is child abuse."

I smirked at Declan's righteous indignation. He'd taken surprising offense to the mandatory college essay workshop the rising seniors had been told to attend. There was no good explanation for why it started so bright and early, or why it couldn't wait until after the first day of school. But so went the life of a teenager: authority figures bossing you around and too many arbitrary rules.

"Vacation's over, son," Gunther drawled from the passenger seat in the way he only did when he was recently-returned from Alabama. For that summer's two-week pilgrimage to his grandmother's house, he'd taken his girlfriend, Zoë. They'd never been outside a fifty-mile radius of one another since they'd gotten together last year, which made them almost as in love as me and Roxy.

"Bo told me all about it," Gunther continued, referring to his older brother, who had graduated three years before. "Special assemblies on college stuff every week. Plus applications. Plus essays. Plus get good grades. Plus college visits. My mom and dad didn't get off his back 'til March."

"Which is exactly why everyone needs to back the hell off now," Declan concluded, still petulant as I meandered my car through the lot. "I mean, at least give us 'till Labor Day. Give us one second to take the best parking spots and push the freshmen around and revel in the fact that we're seniors."

"He's not wrong about the parking spots," Gunther said, sliding his gaze to me before jutting his chin toward the top of the hill. When I focused my sights there, rather than toward the spaces where we'd parked last year, I spotted Zoë's Cayenne.

"Onward and upward," I chimed in. It was a bad pun and a weak platitude to Declan's legitimate complaints. Still, I couldn't help the swell of anticipation that arose. If Zoë's car was here, then Roxy was in tow and I was seconds away from seeing my girl.

Like Zoë and Gunther, Roxy and I had gotten together Junior year and had been equally inseparable. Though, I'd seen her less than I wanted this summer, thanks to us having internships in two different towns. Hers had just ended—a few days after mine —which gave us another week to revel in summer—another week of no homework or alarm clocks or daytime supervision.

"Morning, love," I murmured in her ear a minute later, facing her squarely and angling my gaze to take in her lovely face, which had sprouted light freckles in the summer sun. The sun had also caused her blonde hair to lighten. The combination of the two had given her a bit of a different look, setting off a subtle burst of gold in her tawny eyes. Even this far north, she was every bit a California girl.

"This is bullshit." She pouted. Except, unlike Declan's pouts, Roxy's were cute.

The smile I could never keep from growing when I was around her bloomed as my arms slid around her waist. I hadn't spared a glance at Annika or Zoë in my haste to get to Roxy. Most likely, both were too busy kissing Declan and Gunther to spare a glance at me. We were the three most disgustingly enamored couples in all of Rye.

Coming in at a close fourth, and with twenty-plus years of practice, were my parents: Jack and Elsie Monroe. If there was one thing I'd learned from my mom and dad, it was how to hold on when you found the one. Because when you knew, you just knew. They'd met in their Freshman year at Berkeley when they were only eighteen—barely a year older than Roxy and I were when we met.

Sure, it took us a little while. If I'm honest with myself, I had a crush on her all along—and not just in that half-lustful way that any teenage boy is fascinated with a beautiful girl. It took Declan's meddling on my side, and Zoë's meddling on Roxy's, to get the two of us to realize we were perfect for one another. But every epic love story had a great beginning. We'd be telling ours for the rest of our lives.

"I'd have thought they'd excuse someone with your qualifications from a class as basic as this..." I raised one eyebrow and fixed Roxy with a half-smile. "...seeing as how you're not an amateur anymore."

Roxy tried to elbow me lightly in the ribs as we turned to follow the others. She got embarrassed when I talked about her summer job. Not many teenagers nowadays had worked at a magazine, let alone impressed the editor enough to get themselves published. Roxy had done both and deserved every word of praise.

Everyone knew she was book smart. But Roxy had greatness inside her—one too big for her to see.

Yet, I reminded myself. Roxy didn't know she was great, *yet*. But she would one day. And I would be there when she did.

"After you, my love," I murmured in her ear, uncaring that she'd just attacked my midsection. It would take a whole lot more than that to scare me away.

Before she could get too far, I relieved her of the faded military-canvas messenger bag that hung at her side, pulling it over my own head and arranging the strap across my chest. I kept my hand on the small of her back and held the door for her on our way into the building.

Settling my arm around her shoulders as we walked down the halls, I felt pleasantly possessive as kids we'd barely seen in weeks nodded their hellos. I wasn't one to piss on my territory but it was the first day back and everyone needed to know.

Yup. Roxy's still mine.

"Your place later?" Roxie asked with a muffled yawn.

I waggled my eyebrows a little. "Last Jacuzzi make out of the season."

"But I want to make out all year." Roxy looked dismayed. "Why does summer have to end?"

It *had* been an epic summer—a fermata that held the last notes of our epic junior year— and one I would look back on fondly. But senior year would be just as epic. So would going to UCLA next year with Roxy and being college sweethearts just like my mom and dad.

But that wasn't even the best part. The best part was us living out our dreams—me being a film score composer and Roxy exploring the writing thing and us living in the significantly-warmer sunshine of L.A. Yes, *that* was the very best part: meeting the person you were meant to be with, forever. Being blessed enough to have it all figured out when you were eighteen.

2   READY FOR A FALL

I can't believe
you're the one for me.
If it was this easy to find you,
I should be ready for a fall.
-PJ Olsson, Ready for a Fall

ROXY (EARLY SEPTEMBER)

"Your place or mine?" I asked Jagger breathlessly in-between a series of deep and sugary kisses.

He ignored my question in favor of sucking on my neck, but finally growled, "Mine."

On a picnic table behind the Custard Shack was hardly the place for what I wanted to do with Jagger. But I couldn't be blamed for pouncing on him—not after the way he'd licked ice cream sundae off his spoon.

I'd retaliated, of course—lifted half of a banana from our split with my fingers and locked my eyes on his as I'd cleaned the banana with my tongue. He'd ripped it from my hand and thrown it over his shoulder, pulling me onto his lap. The Custard Shack was days away from closing for the season. We'd gone there every day since school started to get our fill. What I really wanted my fill of now was Jag.

"What time is it?" he asked distractedly, five minutes later, his Tiguan now whizzing down the forest road.

"Time to get a watch," I giggled, enjoying preoccupied, horny Jag. The fact that he didn't just look at the clock on the dashboard told me just how preoccupied. I knew I shouldn't be too hard on him—it was wicked of me to tease when the truth was, I'd been kind of scarce.

Not liking the idea of Jagger and I left alone every day in Rye for the whole summer, my dad had forced me to take an internship with the magazine where my aunt Judy worked part time as a CPA. It held the added bonus of providing me with work experience that would play well on my college applications. So, three days a week, I'd headed to Littleton to earn a few bucks and learn all about the publishing world. And I'd loved it, not least of all for the energy of a busy editorial desk and the feminist slant of the magazine, but because the women I'd worked with were like none I'd ever met.

Until a year ago, I'd been raised by my fickle mother, who'd sold out on providing us with a stable life. She'd struggled to keep up with our rent and to keep money in her pocket. The alimony my dad had paid her to support me, she'd squandered on voice coaching and studio time, all in the name of becoming the next-biggest recording star. She'd never graduated high school and had a series of low-wage, dead-end jobs.

My father, by contrast, had maintained predictable, steady work as a tradesman and turned his once-tiny custom cabinetry shop into a lucrative business. It added up to a big life lesson: learn a practical skill and don't become an artist.

I'd always looked toward college as the first of my hell-will-freeze-over-before-I-become-my-mother insurance policies. I'd never thought about what I wanted to do with my life, beyond that. But working at the magazine had inspired me. It had gotten me thinking about whether writing for a magazine counted as a practical career or a frivolous one. I'd been thinking about it a lot.

Jagger, for his part, had also spent part of his time working, trailing his dad in the ER and cuddling a shitload of babies. That's right—my damn-near perfect boyfriend volunteered as a baby comforter in the NICU. He'd also helped entertain his parents' house guest, who had been a constant fixture in the Monroe home for the past two weeks. It had thrown a serious wrench in our sexy times, but their guest was scheduled to leave that day.

"You think you're funny, do you? Huh?" He reached over the center console to deliver a squeeze to my thigh, one a bit higher than it strictly needed to be. There was something decidedly not-playful about it—a note I'd heard before in his voice and an intensity I'd felt before in his touch. They held a warning that told me he would punish my antics in the most delicious of ways.

I exhaled a shaky breath and shifted my gaze out the window, blind to the scenery that whisked by. Once upon a time, we'd been in favor of taking things slow. Not that fooling around was a curse—even our fully-dressed make-out sessions were phenomenal. But the energy between us had become too great. One day, we'd both just cracked. Jagger and I had been doing the deed since our third week of summer vacation and things between us were sizzling hot.

"Shit," he cursed, snapping me out of my thoughts, and I realized the car had stopped. "They should've been halfway to SFO by now."

As if on cue, Jack Monroe barreled out of the house at a fast clip, car remote in one hand, suitcase in the other.

"We're late," Jack called unnecessarily after Jag and I had exited the Tiguan, then lifted the suitcase to place in the trunk of his black Mercedes. Elsie and her friend sauntered elegantly behind him as he loaded up the car.

"One more hug, dear," called Elsie's friend (was her name Alexis?), opening motherly arms as she took a few steps toward Jagger.

He adjusted himself discreetly behind the Tiguan door before stepping forth to embrace the middle-aged woman and he bent more than he might have strictly needed to for the hug.

"And don't forget what you promised to send," she scolded in a playful but serious tone.

"I won't," smiled Jagger a bit uncomfortably.

"You must be Roxy," she said, surprising me when she turned to extend her hand to me. "I was sorry I didn't have a chance to meet you. *Destinata* is a beautiful piece—I can see Jagger's inspiration."

"Uh...thank you?" I said awkwardly. No one appeared to notice my perplexed expression as the three adults rushed to get in the car. Jack honked the horn as he pulled away, and then it was just me and Jagger.

"They'll be gone 'til dinner," he said devilishly, grabbing my hand and pulling me up to his room.

Hours later, we lay side-by-side, kissing languidly again, this time in the hammock by the warm pool. His father was some sort of soaking enthusiast so, of course, they had three tubs: hot, warm and cold. They were set back from the main house, down a wood-plank path that meandered deeper into his acres-of-forest back-yard and ended in a clearing of trees.

A sturdy cabana and two strung-up hammocks were perfect for lounging, but the main attraction were the soaking pools. All were ovular in shape but the cool one was the largest—a bit too cool for my liking so our default was the warm.

We'd spent practically all our down time this summer in that very spot, though our friends had usually been in tow. The cabana was the biggest space to lounge in and the easiest to get in and out of. But we always gave the cabana to Annika and Declan. Covered by one of the enormous towels the Monroes kept in the space, we swung in the hammock that felt like it had become ours.

Between kisses, I memorized the cupid's bow of his lip, the hue of his hair in sunlight, the vibrant clarity of green-gray eyes. I soaked in the sounds of the forest and loved the sweep of the late summer breeze on my back. I didn't realize I'd fallen asleep until Jagger's whispered words woke me up.

"Destinata...," he had breathed into my hair, barely loudly enough for me to hear.

"What does it mean?" I mumbled groggily, my voice hoarse from disuse.

"My destiny," he murmured, kissing the top of my head. "My world." He kissed me again. "My everything."

I still had trouble, hearing him talk like this, though I knew his words were sincere. I was getting better, but I still couldn't fully accept a love this big.

"Is that Spanish?" I asked. I had no ear for languages. "It sounds like what your mom's friend said to me earlier."

Jagger's body stayed relaxed, but his answering sigh held a certain tension.

"It's Italian. She was referring to your song."

My song has a name?

"How did she hear my song?" I asked, slightly protective of what I liked to think of as exclusive to Jagger and me. He'd started writing it in the early days of our dating and I'd spent countless hours next to him on the piano bench while he fleshed it out. I'd been his sounding board—listening to variation after variation, telling him which elements did and didn't work.

"The day she arrived, I thought I was alone while I was playing it and writing out the sheet music, actually. She took...a professional interest in the piece."

I wrinkled my nose.

"A professional interest? What does she do?"

"She teaches piano—did I not tell you she was my first piano teacher?"

I shook my head.

"What, does she want to teach the piece to her other students?"

This next hesitation was more awkward. It scared me.

He admitted, "Not exactly."

I sat up a little.

"Jagger. You're being vague. And weird. What does she want with you and your song?"

"It's your song, love. And she wants me to study under her again next year. At Juilliard."

I sat straight up then, and spun to face him; he was practically scowling, but I was beaming.

"Jagger, that's amazing! Why aren't you, like, bouncing off the walls?"

He studied me for a moment, searched for something in my face.

"New York's far away, Roxy."

"Yeah, and you're dying to get out of this town. Why aren't you happy about this? We've been talking all summer about getting out of this place."

The expression on his face melted from uncomfortable to strange.

"Getting out, yes..." He seemed cautious as he spoke—as if he were weighing every single word. "Getting out of here together, and going to UCLA".

I blinked, no fewer than five separate thoughts attacking me at once. The milder ones, I might as well have spoken aloud—thoughts like, "But Juilliard is perfect for what you want to do," and, "There's no comparison between Juilliard's music program and the ones at UCLA," and "What kind of idiot turns down an inside track into Juilliard?"

But my other thoughts were not mild—they were ones that whispered at the back of my mind and arose sometimes, unbidden and unwelcome. Thoughts like: "The UCLA plan was always too good to be true." Because we *had* talked about going to UCLA together, just like Declan and Annika had talked about applying to the same mixed bag of schools and Gunther and Zoë had both resolved to go to college together in the South. But it had felt too perfect—too neat and tidy—to actually happen.

I didn't dare speak any of these thoughts aloud. I was thankful that Jag chiming back in gave me a pass on speaking on it further. There was something to be said here, but not today.

"It's my parents' dream, not mine," he said more softly, kissing my hair again. "You saw what you saw today because I haven't told them yet."

"Don't you think you should?" I asked in a tone that wasn't even a little bit elegant.

"Soon, love," he hedged, not looking nearly as confident as he sounded, then channeling someone twice his age. "These things have a way of working themselves out."

3   TICKET TO R DE

I think I'm gonna be sad
I think it's today, yeah
The girl that's driving me mad
Is going away
She's got a ticket to ride
She's got a ticket to ride
She's got a ticket to ride
But she don't care
-The Beatles, *Ticket to Ride*

JAGGER (LATE SEPTEMBER)

The tines of forks and blades of knives scraped against everyday china, filling the not-quite-silence as we ate. *Not-quite*, because our Beatles-only-during-dinner rule was still in effect, though the song was somber and the volume was low. It was peculiar, the way the shuffle function had managed to skip around to every depressing song. The Beatles hadn't recorded that many.

First had come the slow tempo of *Julia*; then the minor key of *For No One*; both songs were about things that dared you to crack a smile. I'd been optimistic when I'd heard the first two bars of *Ticket to Ride*, thinking only that I liked the song—then I remembered the lyrics.

The music voided the chilly silence that had taken over Casa Monroe. We'd all been nippy lately. Roxy was fixated on the Juilliard thing, which meant the too-few times a week we were allowed to study together were spent talking about that. Since "studying together" usually meant "making out", rehashing the Juilliard discussion instead of doing either had me losing out on three fronts.

I'd left her house that afternoon having gotten absolutely no action, having talked no sense into Roxy, and with no homework done, and my friends weren't exactly helping my case. Roxy had leaked the news to Zoe and Annika, which was every bit as good as telling Gunther and Declan directly. Even my boys didn't have my back.

The final straw was my usually-relaxed, even-keeled, California-chill parents turning into bizarro versions of themselves, though every kid in my class was complaining about parental strife. For the first time since the sixth grade, they'd started to nag me about homework and studying for tests, even though I hadn't brought home anything lower than a B+.

The other thing they hadn't nagged me about since I was a kid was practicing my piano. But I played every day without prompting—usually at least twice. They'd put the kibosh on going out on weeknights, which seriously messed with my ability to go to shows, which was my number-one favorite thing to do with Roxy.

"How'd your calculus midterm go?" My mother tried to

sound nonchalant, as if she hadn't been waiting until everyone had been served seconds to ask. The one positive byproduct of this insanity was that my mom—convinced that I needed to eat well to think clearly—had been serving up a steady stream of my dinner favorites.

"I'm predicting an A-," I remarked just as evenly as my mother, chasing my reply with a forkful of cilantro rice.

"They say Mr. Leventhal's tests are pretty hard," my father chimed in. I didn't like the passive-aggressive non-question. What was he implying? That I couldn't deliver yet another A on another hard test?

"I've done fine on his first two." I couldn't help from gritting my teeth a little. And where was my dad getting intel about the difficulty level of my math tests?

"Just remember...there's a lot at stake. You've worked hard all your life. It would be a tragedy to get distracted now."

Only there wasn't a lot at stake. Because I got good grades, had done better-than-great on the SATs, and had the kind of musical talent that would get me into any respectable school. And unlike the kids whose parents were shitting bricks about how to pay for any of this, I could afford it—literally. I'd come into the first installment of my trust fund when I turned eighteen.

"Guys. I've got it under control. My midterms are going well. I've got finished drafts of all my essays and my first deadline is more than a month away. Can you stop treating me like I've already failed?"

My mother had the decency to look a little ashamed. But my father's expression changed in an entirely different way. The look he gave me was sharp. "The Juilliard application is due in two weeks."

Shit.

I hadn't wanted to have this conversation now. I hadn't wanted to have it at all. But I'd changed my mind and everyone needed to know. At some point, I realized my plan to apply to Juilliard and simply decline if I got in did nobody any favors. It would only prolong the false illusion that I might actually go.

"I decided not to apply."

I couldn't deny that it pained me to say the words. Juilliard was something I'd dreamt of, once. I didn't care about the cachet of the big name, but I liked the idea that it was world-class. I might've gone to the website once or thrice. Reading their faculty roster and alumni lists was tantamount to scrolling through a list of musical celebrities.

I regretted the instantaneous horror that slapped my parents faces, but there could be no more beating around the bush. No more keeping the cat in the bag. Better to rip the Band-Aid off and perform any other the-sooner-the-better cliché that would tell them the score.

"You what?" My father hissed at the same time my mother dropped her fork. Her speechlessness was compensated for by my father's only-too-willingness to speak his mind.

"Like hell you're not."

My every teenage instinct commanded me to rage, but my father had taught me well. Remaining calm during an argument was a powerful tool. I'd rehearsed my rationale, tucking it in my back pocket in preparation for this inevitable moment.

"It wouldn't be fair," I said evenly.

"It wouldn't be fair to who?" My mother finally found her voice. I didn't want to take this away from them. I put down my fork, took a long sip of water, and looked directly at my mother.

"To the person who would be more than just honored to be offered a spot. Someone who would actually take it."

"Sweetie, why wouldn't you at least consider it?" But the question irritated me. She'd been using that word a lot: "consider". But that was coded language. It was clear that my parents only tolerated talk about UCLA because they thought to eventually bring me around to their way of thinking. As long as I was "considering" a number of schools, they figured they had a shot. They'd even been working on Roxy, telling her to "consider" NYU's school of journalism.

"Because I want to compose for film scores. And the movie industry is in L.A." It was a perfectly rational argument.

"This is college. Your job isn't to breathe the same air or live on the same street as the people who you want to one day work with—it's to go to the best place to learn."

"If I stay in California, I can do both. Do you know how many composers who are UCLA alumni have won a Grammy or an Academy Award?"

My mother looked at my father then, and my father at my mother. I usually found their silent conversations to be sweet. Not at this exact moment, but in general. Couldn't they see that I just wanted this? To hold onto the one person in the universe who I had my own silent conversations with?

"Enough is enough." My father's voice was grim. His gaze slammed into mine only on the last "enough".

"Jack –" my mother started, but my father cut her off.

"—We're all done pretending this is an about Roxy."

Deadly silence filled the room. Even the music had mysteriously stopped. No hum of the dishwasher or howl of the wind.

"Fine." There was no point in denying it. "I want to go to college with my girlfriend. We both like UCLA. And that's where were going to go."

My dad looked like he might blow a gasket. It was finally time to throw my trump card.

"You guys went to Berkeley and you turned out okay."

My father looked at me sternly. "I went to Berkeley to rebel against my parents. Do you really want to make that comparison?"

My mother leveled a brief glare at my father before turning to me and saying in a much kinder voice, "What your father is saying is that, at your age, he was still finding himself. But you're different—you already know what you want to do."

"And your mother and I *met* at Berkeley, son," my father cut back in. "There's a difference."

He and I stared one another down for a long moment and I queued up my final argument. It was time to take a different tack.

"Alexis is a family friend," I finally pointed out. "We shouldn't have her pulling strings if it's an offer I'm not going to take."

My parents looked at one another again.

"It's not the idea of UCLA that bothers us." My father kept his gaze on my mother for a beat too long before shifting it to me. "It's the fact that you never talked about UCLA before. We're not telling you what we want you to do. We're asking you to take more time to decide, and that means not shutting any doors."

This time, as my father and I stared at one another, something vulnerable replaced the anger in his eyes. Something about my plan had my parents deeply worried.

"A year is a long time," my dad continued with caution. "A lot of things can change. A year ago, you weren't even dating Roxy."

His implication stole my breath and punched me in the gut.

"In a year, you may feel differently about Juilliard," my mom took up. They were a united front. "We just don't want you to close that door."

I fucking hate this.

"What about Alexis?" I gritted out finally.

"If we burn a bridge with Alexis, it's on me," My father piped back in. "I'll let her know you're undecided. But the Juilliard deadline is in two weeks. So please...please, just apply."

4 THE MIDDLE

Hey, don't write yourself off yet.
It's only in your head, you feel left out
or looked down on.
Just try your best, try everything you can.
Don't you worry what they tell themselves
when you're away.
-Jimmy Eat World, The Middle

ROXY (EARLY OCTOBER)

"Rox?"

My dad's voice broke me out of my Jag-filled thoughts as it sliced across the voice of actual Jag. I was supposed to be mapping out the construction of my balsa wood bridge for physics—not using homework time to flirt with my boyfriend on the phone.

"In here, Dad," I called. Not that he didn't know that if I wasn't in the kitchen or the laundry room or watching TV downstairs, that I would be in my room, and that if my backpack was in its usual spot downstairs, I was definitely home.

"Shit, Jag. It's my dad. He's home early. I gotta go."

I hung up abruptly, knowing Jag wouldn't take it as a snub. Both of us were already on watch from our respective parents, who'd told us to scale down the nightly calls for the sake of getting our homework done. Such rules had been implemented so close together and with such striking similarity as to rouse suspicion. I'd wondered whether my own dad and Jag Monroe's parents had been in cahoots.

Jag and I had been busy debating whether the best Metallica ballad was either of the obvious choices—*Nothing Else Matters* or *The Unforgiven*—versus the far-more obscure but more lyrically-cryptic *Low Man's Lyric*. Jag, as usual, was arguing the unsung heroism of the more obscure song, which was, in my opinion, a bit too much of a dirge. But we'd have to settle the matter later and I'd have to put my phone away quickly. It was time for me to deal with my dad.

Everyone in our crowd agreed that our parents were going a little crazy. Even Zoe's absentee parents seemed to have reengaged. By the first day of school, they'd returned from one of their many trips abroad, given her housekeeper-slash-nanny, Neide, the month off, and announced plans to stay a while.

I opened my book quickly, picked up my pencil, and placed my finger on the paragraph where I'd left off, appearing to trace words for good measure. I wasn't really blowing off my homework, and had to make sure it didn't look that way. I would've gotten it done after I got off the phone with Jagger.

My father's footsteps neared, plodding up newly-installed bamboo steps at a fast clip and with a distinct thud that told me he still had on his shop boots. Just when I thought I was in the clear—fully ready for him to burst in, the screen of my cell phone lit up again with a message from Jag.

Text me later. With an "s".

I tipped my face downward and smiled into my book. My dad wasn't stupid. And my blushing would probably be a dead giveaway that I'd just been talking to Jag. But when he walked into the room, he didn't do his standard look-around that always felt like a spot inspection.

"You want to tell me what this is?"

My dad was looking at me pointedly, and holding something in his hand. I could only hope that it wasn't anything incriminating, like ticket stubs from that concert Jag had taken me to last week in Sonoma when I'd told my dad I was at Zoe's. Or, worse, the dreaded doomsday scenario: finding my birth control pills—anything that could lead to long-term grounding.

"What is what?" I asked as innocently as possible, trying to look as if I had been captivated by studying the weight-bearing capacities of various woods.

He finally brought his hand forward—too quickly for me to see what he held—and punctuated his next words by slapping the object down on top of my book. It was a college brochure from Brown.

"This."

The single word held accusation, as if possessing a college brochure were a crime. Possessing one from Brown might as well have been. In my defense, I hadn't ordered it. But I knew it was out of my league. Even if the long shot scenario happened and I got in, Brown cost a shit-ton of money. And we didn't have anything close to a shit-ton.

It was one thing if I'd wanted to become an investment banker or a brain surgeon or something that gave me a snowball's chance in hell of paying off sizable student loans. But there was a chance I'd have to live on a writer's salary.

"Oh, that?" I relaxed when I realized it wasn't contraband.

"Yeah, they just sent it to me out of the blue. That's why I threw it away."

"Why would you do that, Rox?" he demanded.

I just blinked up at him, because he should already know why.

"They didn't *just send it to you*," he said with emphasis. "I ordered an information packet."

"You—" I sputtered, not even able to finish. Why would my dad do that?

"They have the best writing program in the country, Rox. And you haven't stopped talking about writing since you got that summer job. Why wouldn't you try to get in?"

His eyebrows knitted together. What had initially looked to me like his semi-angry "you're in trouble, kid" look, I had mistaken for his incredulous one. A sinking feeling came over me as I realize what I was dealing with here, something I should have anticipated might manifest in this way: extreme parental pride.

My dad believed in me. So much so, that he thought I could get in to Brown. So much so, that he thought they'd give me money to attend. I loved that my dad was so proud of me. But he'd never gone to college, and I didn't think he understood just how complicated all of it was.

"Dad, I can't get in to Brown..."

His hand went to his hip and his disbelieving look turned into his indignant one. "Uh-uh. Don't sell yourself short."

"It's really, really hard, Dad. You know that kid, Xandra Morris, the valedictorian from last year, who was, like the smartest kid in the class and a National Merit Scholar and all that business? She didn't even get in to Brown and she got into all the other Ivies."

"I don't care what Xandra Morris did, Rox. I'm talking about you. And you've got a shot at Brown. So take this...and read it. Okay?"

The faintest welling of tears sprung to my eyes. I didn't want to have to say what was on my mind. Luke Vega was a proud man. He'd worked hard to pay my mother alimony. He did very well now, but my mother getting so much for all those years still meant that we weren't rich. He'd never be able to afford any of the big mansions in the hills where Jag and Zoe lived. He'd lived in the same old very middle-class house I remembered all my life.

"Dad, I'm just gonna go to one of the UC schools. It's the best state university system in the country, and it's a lot cheaper than any Ivy. I'm gonna look at UCLA, UCSB and Irvine. LA is where I want to be. That's where the music scene is. And you know I want to write about music."

My father narrowed his eyes suspiciously. "This had better not be about Jagger."

It took a little acting on my part to seem outraged. My dad didn't need to know that Jag and I had been talking about UCLA for months. He liked Jag well enough, but he didn't like the idea of high school sweethearts. I mean, look at how things turned out for him and my mom.

"What, Dad??! No!"

"Is he applying to UCLA?"

"Dad...it's California. Everyone's applying to the UC schools," I hedged with an eye roll.

"I thought his parents would've wanted him to go to Harvard or Yale or something," my dad said with less judgment than I expected.

Try Juilliard, I said to myself, and ignored the sadness I felt at the idea.

"Jag wants to be in the music business, too. There's no music business in Cambridge or New Haven," I hedged. I would do it subtly, but I had to leave room for the possibility that we would end up at the same school.

"Quit throwing away college brochures, Rox. I've done my

research. A lot of the schools use the common application. It won't take you much effort to apply to a few more."

"But –" I vainly protested.

"And, don't worry about the money. You go to any school that you want."

Whatever protest had nearly flown out of my mouth stopped the second I heard my father's words.

"What do you mean, don't worry about money? Dad...you have no idea how much some of the schools cost."

He shook his head a little, chuckled, and smiled for the first time since he'd walked into the room. "Baby, I've known how much college costs for more than ten years. Brown costs $50,000 for tuition and just over $15,000 for room and board. Add inn that you'd need an allowance of $500 a month and that you'll be there for four years, we're looking at about $285,000."

My heart beat out of my chest and I felt short of breath. It winded me to speak. "How do you even know that?"

It was then that I saw the pride in his eyes.

"Because I've been saving up for your college since you were eight."

I think my heart stopped then. I turned the words over in my head.

I've been saving up for your college since you were eight.

Tears blurred my vision. And then I was in my father's arms and sobbing into his shoulder. And I didn't know why I was crying, because I hadn't even hoped for this.

Later, it hit me, after my dad and I went to the diner to eat, after I finished studying, did some laundry, and avoided texting with Jag. I wasn't ready to share news I could barely fathom myself. I couldn't tell him yet that everything had changed.

5 ANOTHER BRICK IN THE WALL

We don't need no education.
We don't need no thought control
No dark sarcasm in the classroom.
Teachers, leave them kids alone.
Hey! Teachers! Leave them kids alone...
**-Pink Floyd, *Another Brick in the Wall*
(Part 2)**

JAGGER (LATE OCTOBER)

Principal Wyatt took to the stage to weak applause, and not just because the crowd was small with only the seniors at assembly. The woman was notorious for long, preachy lectures full of old-school ideas. Principal Wyatt herself was over seventy and every bit as ornery as any other septuagenarian. She was thin, wore skirt suits and drank coffee all day at her desk. No one had ever seen her eat.

But she was an icon in the town and a fixture in the school—

she'd even taught Roxy's parents. By all accounts, she'd been gray-haired and stern-faced even then. According to Mrs. Convery's intro, Wyatt was going to give us some sort of pep talk about college. So far, senior year had found us spending an inordinate amount of time on such things: logistical primers and motivational speeches; sports games and homecoming rallies....

Trinity High and its frigging pep, I thought, wistful once again for my far-simpler underclassmen days.

Wyatt's heels clickety-clacked across the stage and she took her place behind the podium, glaring out at the crowd from behind thick glasses. She was also famous for dramatic silences and her ability to stare down a crowd. Come to think of it, I wasn't sure I'd ever seen her blink.

"One million dollars," she finally began in a booming voice and staccato rhythm. "Can any of you tell me what that number should mean to you right now?"

No one ever answered her rhetorical questions, but that never stopped her from these sorts of quizzes.

"Anyone?" she probed, sweeping her gaze over the crowd.

"The money I'd pay someone to get out of this assembly," a kid behind me muttered. Wyatt's gaze snapped sharply toward the small eruption of snickers.

"Oh, this is funny, is it?" She asked in a lighter voice, with a put-on smile. "Go ahead and crack wise. Treat college like a joke. Let's see how hard you're laughing when your gar gets repossessed, you're behind on your rent, and you can't do anything to help your situation."

The room quieted again, and she went back to her sweeping glare. "Oh. Have I got your attention? Well, listen up, and listen good. One million dollars is the average incremental salary you'll earn over your lifetime if you attend college versus if you don't. That's more than $30,000 annually if you work for twenty-five years."

And, so began her diatribe. It was a push for us all to leave Rye and consider applying to college, never mind that Wyatt herself still lived in the house that she grew up in, having spent all except her own college years within the confines of the town. I rolled my eyes for how much of a joke all of this was.

Rye was the kind of Northern California town where people like my parents came to escape the rat race. By all other accounts, it was declining. It had been populated during the Gold Rush, and had mainly survived on camping tourism and logging over the past century. Wyatt was preaching to the choir. Even the kids who might return to Rye wanted at least to sow their wild oats at one of the UCs.

"It wasn't so long ago that I was your age, " Wyatt droned on, minutes later. "You think I've never heard of *senioritis*?" she challenged.

I caught Gunther's face out of the corner of my eye. "Not so long ago?" he mouthed and gave an incredulous look. Unintentionally, I laughed out loud. It earned me a sharp look from Mr. Taylor, which careened me back into irritation. They'd pushed our lunch period back for this? This assembly was boring as hell, and I was starting to get hangry. I slid my hand in my pocket and pulled out a piece of Big Red, folding it into my mouth as I tuned out the speech and looked around.

Gunther's head was now bowed toward his lap, his eyes alight with attention, which convinced me he was sexting with Zoë. My eyes scanned the auditorium until they settled on spiky blue hair. The blush on her face told me I was exactly right. A couple rows back from Zoë were Declan and Annika. She was feigning attention, but he wasn't even trying. His baseball cap was pulled low over his eyes and he was fast asleep.

"A mind is a terrible thing to waste," Wyatt's voice boomed, interrupting my thoughts.

Really? The UNCF tagline?

Gunther stopped texting long enough to look over at me, eyebrow raised. I shook my head in silent solidarity. I glanced over at Roxy then, sure she'd be cracking up at Wyatt's theatrics.

But she wasn't. My girl was rapt with attention, as serious a look as I'd ever seen on her face. It wiped the smile off of mine. Ever since her dad had done the big reveal on the pile of money he'd squirreled away, the way she acted any time someone talked about college had changed. I knew I should be happy for her. I *was* happy for her. But I was disappointed in myself. Because it had never occurred to me that our UCLA plan pivoted on anything having to do with money.

My discomfort about the matter followed me to lunch. Roxy and I had changed our plan—kind of. I would apply to a few other music programs and she, too, would branch out from only applying to UCs. It was a logical resolution—what kid in this day and age didn't hedge his bets?—and probably naïve of me to ever have thought either of us would get away with applying to only two schools.

"When do you head to New York, dude?" Declan asked, sliding into the cafeteria chair with an alarmingly-full tray.

"It's supposed to be next week," I mumbled, stuffing a fry into my mouth.

"*Supposed* to be?" Zoë piped up. "You mean your Juilliard audition isn't totally confirmed?"

"No, it is..." I admitted, "I'm just still not sure I want to go."

Declan, Annika, and Zoë all stopped eating and looked up at me in shock. Roxy was still getting her lunch, thank God—this was a contentious, and, unfortunately, a recurring conversation. Berklee School of Music was another formidable east coast choice and they offered a Bachelors in Composition. Boston was only an hour away from Providence, which would work out well if Roxy ended up at Brown.

"Why wouldn't you want to audition at Juilliard?" Annika demanded.

"Yes, Jagger—why wouldn't you?" came Roxy's voice from behind me.

Guess she wasn't as far away as I thought.

"I just want to keep my options open," I lobbied, now channeling my parents and silently hoping for the other girls' support. "My mom's taking me to see other schools while we're on the east coast. It's not like Juilliard has the only composition program in the nation."

"It has the best," Roxy scoffed unhelpfully.

"Actually, Yale's been ranked higher for the past few years," Gunther stated, throwing me a supportive glance. Yale's program was graduate only but I wouldn't mention that. I appreciated that at least one person had switched to my corner.

"Speaking of college..." I changed the subject and rummaged in my bag to pull out printouts for Annika and Declan. "My mom and dad got confirmation their references were received."

My dad was Chief of Medicine at the hospital and had written a professional reference for Annika based on her volunteer work in the nursery as a cuddler. My mom had written a personal reference for Declan, attesting to his passion for architecture. They were both hoping that these references would tip the scales in their favor for their first choice and my parents' alma mater. Declan wanted an engineering program with a strong design focus and Annika would focus on political and social justice—she wanted to go pre-law.

Zoë, as it turned out, was originally from Louisiana, and shared Gunther's obsession with the south. He was interested in Civil War studies, and she was undecided. Together, they'd apply to Tulane, Duke, and a few other schools in Texas that I hadn't really heard of.

Then there was Roxy. Brown had opened the floodgates for

her to look at more east coast writing programs. So far, she liked Williams, Middlebury and Brown. That "little" op/ed she'd written near the end of her internship had finally been published. It had even gotten picked up for syndication by the Huffington Post. Between that, and the stellar recommendation from the magazine's Editor-in-Chief, her application to any writing program would be oozing with cred.

"This is gonna be so sweet if it works out." Declan looked excited as he plucked the confirmation printout from my hand, pausing his enthusiastic devouring of the contents of his lunch tray long enough to inspect the paper. "Send your mom my thanks."

Annika threw him a look and he started in a way that implied she'd just kicked him under the table.

"Thank her yourself, you idiot," she scolded. "As in, send a note."

"Seriously, babe..." Declan ignored her chastisement and put his arm around her shoulder. "We're taking them out to dinner when we both get in."

"And the six of us should throw a party to celebrate!" Zoë clapped excitedly as she beamed around the table. "You know... on March 10th."

Decision day was a day I was already dreading. My attention darted to Roxy, who also didn't look nearly as excited as Annika, Declan or Zoë. The ever-perceptive Gunther surveyed the table, looking as nervous as I felt.

"Alright, change of subject," he said with lightness in his voice, though he was looking at me when he said it. "We got plenty of it from Wyatt. Enough of this college talk."

6 BATTLEFIELD

I never meant to start a war
You know, I never wanna hurt you
Don't even know what we are fighting for
Why does love always feel like
a battlefield, a battlefield, a battlefield?
-Jordyn Sparks, Battlefield

JAGGER (EARLY NOVEMBER)

"Mr. Vega!"

Upon seeing Roxy's dad, my slow pacing faltered for a beat. It was rare to see anyone other than patients in the hospital's maternity gardens. The secluded, glass-encased solarium was on the same floor as the maternity ward. I'd thought myself alone, though it wasn't uncommon for me to see new moms walking slowly as their recovering bodies healed, or spending time with their older children. Today I was cuddling Claire, whose own mother had two older kids at home.

But apparently, I wasn't alone because Luke Vega was ambling toward me.

"You scared the dickens out of me," I remarked with a little laugh that I hoped sounded a lot less nervous then Luke Vega made me. Also, when I said that sentence in my head, I hadn't used the word "dickens"—I'd used the words, "ever-loving shit."

But Mr. Vega remained quiet until he was much closer to my space, and smiled a half smile before saying, "Wouldn't want to do that...."

Before I could consider some punitive reason for his visit— like if he'd found out about that concert I'd taken Roxy to that night she was supposed to be at Zoë's, or about that time we'd cut school to go up the coast—a terrifying thought occurred: Luke Vega, who had never sought me out, had somehow found me at work. Why would he be in the hospital if he wasn't visiting someone sick?

"Is Roxy okay, sir? I mean... Is she here for some reason?"

Mr. Vega frowned for a couple of seconds before his face softened in understanding.

"No, no... Roxy's fine."

I exhaled a sigh of relief and resumed my slow pacing the moment I felt a little wiggle in my arms from baby Claire. I looked down at her then.

Don't worry, I telegraphed with my eyes. *Roxy's okay.*

All of the babies I cuddled liked to hear about Roxy. Before I'd met her, I'd sometimes sing the babies I cuddled songs or talked about my favorite bands. I'd always had a way with the little ones, but I'd noticed specifically that we all felt better when I got to talking about my girl.

"I knew you volunteered here..." Mr. Vega looked down at the bundle in my arms, but his expression remained neutral. "...with the babies."

I smiled then, eager, as always, to win points with Roxy's dad.

"Yes, sir. I'm a cuddler."

Mr. Vega made a sound halfway between a hum and a harrumph before asking, "You like babies, do you?"

"Yes sir. I do." I stood a little prouder. Judging from the reactions I got from most people who found out, serving as a volunteer cuddler at the hospital was a shining feather in my cap. You had to pass a criminal background check, undergo extensive training, and be able to handle the most fragile and precious of lives. Do you think most other teenagers could claim this? That was a definite no.

"Well, you'd better not like them too much," he said in a bit of a growl, leaning closer and narrowing his eyes in a way that found me taking a step back. It only took that long for me to understand his meaning.

"Oh, no!" I insisted quickly. "I meant that I like other people's babies. I am far too young to have babies of my own, sir. I wasn't talking about wanting a baby with Roxy. Not that I would judge anybody who had a baby at seventeen, because I know that's how old you were when Roxy was born, Mr. Vega, and she's just about perfect."

Holy hell, I screamed internally. *Shut the fuck up, Jagger*. I looked down at Claire, hoping for some show of solidarity. She looked sleepy, so not much help. But at least appearing to check on her gave me a chance to stop and catch my breath.

"What I mean is, sir, that I respect the fact that you had Roxy young. But I don't think that's the right path for her and me. It'll be a long time before we start a family."

But Mr. Vega didn't look relieved—not completely relieved, at least. His already unreadable-expression became more complex.

"That's what I'm here to talk to you about. I knew from Roxy that you volunteer here on Tuesdays and Thursdays." Mr. Vega motioned toward a sticker that was affixed to the hem of his shirt. I hadn't noticed it before. "I know a nurse."

Well, that explains that. Roxy had mentioned that her dad was seeing a woman. I had no problem with Luke Vega getting out more, which meant less supervision for me and Roxy.

"I've known Sadie since I was little," I said with a smile, surmising that Luke's "friend" was neither Carol or Sylvia, the other two maternity nurses on desk duty that day, who were both married. "She's really nice."

"Well, I'm glad you approve." Roxy got her sarcasm from her father. "But I'm not here to talk about me—I'm here to talk about you."

"Oh?" I still didn't know what he was doing here, but I was ready to get to the point. "Have I done something wrong?"

"I don't know, Jagger. Have you?" He asked with an eyebrow raised.

I'd grown three inches over the summer, which made us the same height, but he was still a big man, and he had an imposing energy about him. I sometimes mused that if he hadn't become a woodworker, he ought to have become a cop.

"I never want to do anything wrong in your eyes, sir," I replied instead of lying directly. It wasn't untrue, but Roxy and I were teenagers – sometimes we broke the rules. But if Luke Vega was going to be my future father-in-law, I needed him to like me.

"What are your intentions with my daughter, Jagger?"

My heart raced at the question. I had expected such a conversation, only, not so soon. And I'd expected to initiate it—had expected to ask for Roxy's hand in marriage sooner than anyone thought.

"You know that I love your daughter, sir..." I had told him this myself. After last year's unfortunate incident that involved me lying to Roxy and then paying the price, I'd spent several nights shivering under a blanket and sleeping on the Vega porch. When Mr. Vega told me she wouldn't speak to me, I'd respectfully asked that he let me stay so that I could show Roxy how much I loved her.

"Yeah... I got that," he replied.

"And I'd like to spend the rest of my life with her," I blurted out.

I straightened a little then, even as I bounced little Claire, more than capable of multitasking with a baby in my arms. Before he could protest, I sallied forth with haste. "But I know we're way too young to get married. So that's not for now. It's for someday. But, Mr. Vega, I *will* ask."

I wanted to be respectful, but I also wanted him to know that I was serious, and that I was grown enough to have my own plans.

"And, just when is someday, according to your timeline?" He crossed his arms in front of him.

I stood my ground. "After we graduate college."

"And you'll still be together after college?" he goaded.

"Yes we will, sir. I don't plan on us ever breaking up."

Mr. Vega put his other hand on his hip then, pursed his lips, and looked down at the ground for a silent moment.

Whatever he was going to say next, it scared the bejesus out of me, but I liked that Luke Vega was a straight shooter.

"I was you once, kid—so in love I couldn't walk straight. So sure of my future with Star, I had it all mapped out. Wanna know what it looked like?"

I nodded A hint of something wistful whispered at Mr. Vega's voice and for a fleeting second I saw it clearly: the loss in his eyes.

"Before Roxy..." he began with emphasis, "...we talked about going to Nashville. I played the guitar and Star sang and each of us was gonna do a little of both. You know—me writing songs for other people, her performing songs as a solo artist, and us having a singer/songwriter act we performed together."

I listened intently. Roxy didn't talk very much about her

parents' relationship, though I knew that Luke and Star were estranged. I'd endured one awkward dinner with Roxy and her mom that summer, after Star had dropped her back off in Rye following her two-week's visitation. Things between Roxy and her mother were pretty chilly. And when Star had asked me nonstop about my mother's music business ties, things had gotten a little weird.

"Then we got pregnant," Luke continued. Only, when he said it, he didn't sound grim. He said it like it was the best thing that had ever happened to him.

"And I knew we could still have the dream. Even if it took us a little longer than planned. You ever hear Star sing?"

I shook my head.

"You wouldn't know it from looking at her career now, but she had talent. Back then, I was confident—too confident—that both of us would make it in the music business. In hindsight, I'm the one who would've gotten chewed up and spit out. And I'd have been okay with things if I never made it. But Star...she really had a shot."

I still didn't know what all of this had to do with me and Roxy, but I wanted Mr. Vega to tell me more. It seemed uncharitable to ask why Star hadn't broken through, seeing as how she'd taken Roxy and left Luke to go after said shot. I spit out the most intelligent question I could think of in the hopes that he would keep on.

"Is that why you didn't take yours?" Jagger wanted to know. "You realized you didn't want it bad enough?"

Luke shook his head. "See...me and Star always talked like we wanted the same thing—like the music was it. But when it came down to it, it wasn't the music I wanted—it was her."

Jag let the words set in, knowing Luke Vega was trying to teach him some sort of lesson. But, Jagger didn't see what.

Because, of course Luke had wanted Star. He and Star had been in love and she was the prize.

"What I failed to realize..." Luke continued, "...until it was too late, was that, no matter how alike our dreams might have sounded, they weren't the same. Star wanted music first. The other blessings meant nothing if music didn't come first, but for me—"

I didn't mean to cut Mr. Vega off. "—Star and Roxy were your blessings."

I thought about this for a long time.

"Look, kid. I don't want to burst your bubble. I know you love my daughter. And, to tell you the truth, part of me likes the idea of the two of you going to college together. Of her having a good kid like you looking out for her. You think I like the idea of my single, eighteen-year-old daughter going to college parties alone?"

Suddenly, Mr. Vega looked as sick as I felt.

"Mr. Vega...are you suggesting that Roxy and I break up?"

Mr. Vega shook his head slowly, seeming to be careful as he chose his words. "I'm coming to you directly, even though Roxy would cold shoulder me for a year if she found out what I was doing. I'm coming here to say—no matter what she says and how short she sells herself sometimes—beneath all of that, Roxy has dreams.

"Part of that's my fault...letting things get too far with her mother in L.A... She doesn't know what she's capable of right now, and she doesn't know how bad she wants it. But the day she does will come. And I don't want anything to stand in her way."

"I understand, sir." My words sounded stoic even to my own ears. I suddenly felt stiff. I didn't 100% understand what he wanted me to do, but I got the gist. "And I do appreciate you coming to me, man-to-man," I added on with sincerity then.

But Luke didn't leave, even though could have and maybe

even should have, and maybe even like I wanted him to. His tone was apologetic when he spoke.

"I know when you're young, you think everything's gonna turn out alright. And maybe it will. Roxy says your parents met in college and they've been happily married ever since. But, take it from me. It could go the other way."

I was quiet again. By then, Claire had fallen fast asleep, unable to be bothered by such serious afternoon talk.

"If you had to do it all over again..." I trailed off, not finishing the question he knew I was asking.

"Star and I would have ended up friends—might even have ended up together—if I hadn't held on so tight."

7 LOVE IS A BATTLEFIELD

You're begging me to go,
then making me stay.
Why do you hurt me so bad?
It would help me to know,
do I stand in your way?
Or am I the best thing you've had?
-Pat Benatar, Love is a Battlefield

Jagger (Late November)

Send me a happy song, I texted Roxy after dinner, grateful for the sanctuary of my room. I was sprawled, face up, on my bed, seconds away from pressing what I'd started referring to as "her pillow" to my face. Days after she'd been here, it still held the faint aroma of her shampoo.

Uh-oh, what happened? She texted back. I'd just endured another tense dinner. I tapped out the one word that would tell her everything she needed to know:

Parents.

Midterms or piano? She shot back quickly. She knew they'd been on my case. But I hedged, because Roxy didn't need to know my parents had put her at the center of my war over Juilliard.

Both.

I waited for her text, but instead, my phone rang. I didn't need to speak a greeting.

"You're so lucky your dad's cool about grades," I groused, detecting the slosh of water in the background. I pictured her standing in her kitchen, washing dishes.

"Yeah, well the bar's a lot lower for me," she said at the same time the sink turned on. "By the time he was our age, he'd dropped out of high school and had a kid."

Something about her comment made me uncomfortable, even though it was all true: Roxy's dad *was* cooler about studying than my parents. Maybe that was because Roxy came home with straight As and he wasn't going to badger her to fix something that wasn't broken. But never once had he telegraphed low expectations of his daughter. I couldn't tell Roxy about our talk at the hospital, of course, but I still wished I had a way to get through. There was a way Roxy talked about her prospects sometimes that I didn't like.

"When can you get out of jail?" I asked, instead of bringing any of that up. I couldn't handle another tough conversation.

The water cut off. "Not 'til Friday night."

Roxy sounded disappointed. Not as disappointed as me. If there was one thing Luke Vega was a hard-ass about, it was making sure I didn't have unfettered access to his daughter. To him, that meant absolutely no going out during the week. He was already suspicious about the study group we did at Annika's house on Tuesday nights. Nowadays, I mainly saw Roxy at school.

"But you're still clear for Journey weekend, right?" I had to double-check. Having something amazing to look forward to was the only thing that would keep me sane. Journey was playing AT&T Park and Foreigner was opening for them. It was a long enough drive to San Francisco that we'd have to stay the night. Mr. Vega had almost vetoed the trip. But my parents had saved it, arranging for us to stay the night in the totally-supervised and apparently enormous apartment of my mother's friend.

"It's only a month away, not that I'm counting the days." Roxy's weary little chuckle gave me comfort. It told me she hated all of this as much as me.

I was about to tell her I'd ordered us original vintage band T-shirts from Journey's Escape Tour in the '80s, when I heard a knock on the door.

"Jag, honey?" came a gentle voice from the hallway.

"Shit," I told Roxy. "It's my mom. I gotta go. I'll call you later, love." We were used to hasty goodbyes, though I preferred our lengthier, sweeter ones.

Pulling myself up off my bed, I crossed the room to let my mother in. No doubt, she was here to check that I was okay after the argument over dinner. My dad would come around, but not until he'd brooded for a while. But my mom liked to mend fences right away.

"Dad knows he was wrong," she began straightaway.

Dad knows he was an asshole, I kept to myself. I'd been a bit of an asshole, too. Despite the long list of items I had acquiesced to, the college situation continued to escalate. My dad didn't like that every place where I applied came with a plan for how Roxy and I could be together. He also didn't like that I kept pointing out our friends were doing the same thing.

"I think we owe each other an apology," I conceded. "Neither of us should've gotten so angry."

"Well...your father does an excellent job of coming off as angry when he's really scared."

This was the part I didn't get. "Scared of what?" I had to know. "It's not like Roxy and I are running off to join the circus."

She shook her head and looked mildly disappointed.

"Just because you're eighteen doesn't mean our instinct to protect you magically disappears. He's scared of letting you make a mistake you'll regret."

I quieted, because I knew this. I just didn't understand why they were so specifically invested when I would be fine either way.

"What we know, that you don't..." my mother continued, "...is that there's a dark side to sacrifice. You see how we are now, after we made it through our struggles. But we nearly broke up, your father and I."

"I know," I said a bit impatiently, "I remember, when I was little...the summer you shipped me off to my cousins in Alaska." It was just after my baby brother had passed away—a terrible time for everyone. I didn't understand what any of it had to do with sacrifice.

"Twice, then..." my mother revised, throwing me a matter-of-fact look. "Love's messier than you think."

I didn't need to ask the question out loud. My eyes must've said it all: *why?*

"If you add it up, the truth was, we were just too young."

"Everyone keeps saying that," I said with as little frustration as I could. "Like being young is some kind of curse. But no one says what being "too young" really means."

I realized how truly I'd been waiting for this—some specific objection to me and Roxy's plan.

She was quiet for a minute. I could tell from my mom's look on her face that I wouldn't like whatever she said next. It didn't stop her from asking. Because, unlike my father's way, which was to tell, hers was to ask.

"I'm not saying I think this will happen, but have you thought of what UCLA might be like if the two of you broke up?"

I knew she wasn't really looking for an answer. I didn't think that we would break up. But my mom was right—without Roxy at UCLA, I'd be lost.

"I know Roxy's from Los Angeles. She's mentioned that's one reason why she wants to go back. But have you ever met her friends? Or thought about what it will be like for the two of you when you go to a place where she knows people and you don't?"

It was another question I had thought about—another question I hadn't wanted to, a clear signal that I probably should.

"Now, picture yourself at Juilliard. Pretend Roxy had a reason to go there and that the two of you were there instead of UCLA. Now ask yourself the same question: if you broke it off, but you still got to go to Juilliard, would it feel like everything would be okay?"

But I couldn't take any more of her questions. "I'm gonna make mistakes, Mom."

She nodded. "I know you will. But some mistakes have bigger consequences than others. Being young means being ignorant, in the literal sense of the word. No one's saying you haven't thought it through, or that you're being stupid. But there are things you can't know about yourself, or about her, or about what you really want from the world until you've gone out on your own and lived in it."

"I see your point, but..." I let out a heavy sigh, still not knowing how to get through to her. "They're still my mistakes to make."

She nodded again. "They are. But life is long and regrets can eat at you forever. I regret following your dad to Minnesota for his residency."

The sentiment surprised me, because I'd never heard her talk about their years in Minnesota that way. Though, as I thought about it, I realized she never talked about them fondly.

"It was a great opportunity for him—the Mayo Clinic—but it was career suicide for me. I gave up a great job at a studio in Oakland. I was building my reputation, I had people who knew me...I was even starting to get some gigs in L.A."

"So why didn't dad just do his residency someplace else?"

"Because that's not how residencies work, and that's not how relationships work, either, and I didn't know back then how to advocate for what I needed."

I frowned. "I don't understand. Why would Dad be okay with going to Minnesota if you had to make a choice like that?"

My mother looked at me pointedly. "Like I said, I don't think it was the right decision. Thirty-year-old us wouldn't have made that decision. But, twenty-three-year-old us did. We didn't have the tools to navigate the imbalance in our power dynamic and other things that were going on."

My mother and I had a great relationship, but she'd never spoken to me about such things. I knew at that moment, we were about to have a very different kind of a talk.

"What power dynamics?" I had to know.

"Things I didn't think had to matter, but they did. His money. My gender. How starting a family would mean different things for each of us. And what those things should have meant for our choices. You think the only person we're watching out for here is you—that this is about us wanting the very best for our son. You forget...I was Roxy once."

It was the last thing I'd expected my mother to say, but when she did, some of the puzzle pieces came together.

"Have you ever even considered that UCLA may not be where Roxy belongs?" she asked sensibly.

I admitted something I wouldn't have in front of my father. "UCLA was her idea."

"Roxy doesn't think like you. And she's never had the same choices. Right now, she's doing what every other kid in California is doing and applying to UC schools. But when the moment comes when she knows her potential, she may not want what either of you think. Right now, her dreams only stretch as far as she can see."

I thought about this for a long, long time. I thought about it for minutes. Wasn't it me who always chided her for not understanding her worth? My mother was right, but so was I. Roxy *would* see herself differently one day. But we loved each other too fiercely to let go.

"I can't control when or how that happens," I said. "I understand what you're saying, but I can't solve for that."

"No, you can't," my mother agreed. "But college can."

I turned the words over and over in my mind, even as she continued to speak.

"I have no regrets about loving your father, Jag, but I also have no illusions," she concluded. "Committing to one another when we were so young held me back."

8 LOVESONG

Whenever I'm alone with you,
you make me feel like I am home again.
Whenever I'm alone with you,
you make me feel like I am whole again.
Whenever I'm alone with you,
you make me feel like I am young again.
Whenever I'm alone with you,
you make me feel like I am fun again.
-The Cure, Lovesong

ROXY (EARLY DECEMBER)

"Is a blindfold really necessary?"

In my mind's eye, I could see Jag smirk. Since my senses were restricted, the only tangible thing I had to latch on to was his shifting of gears. It was an odd sensation—his Tiguan was automatic, but the car we were in now had manual transmission.

Wherever we were going, it was a special-enough occasion to take his dad's Mercedes.

It wasn't our official anniversary—not the one we'd said we'd count, at least. We'd decided that our real anniversary would be the one that marked the date after we'd both come clean. The Instagram friend request debacle had led to two months of topsy-turvy—some of it spent in halcyon bliss, some of it spent fighting, and the rest spent somewhere in between. We'd gotten together for real after we'd worked past our bullshit, and come in free and clear and in good faith. But that was another story.

Still, I'd wracked my brain for other possibilities. I'd scoured the internet for the tour dates of all of my favorite bands. Most likely, Jag was taking me to a show. Going to shows was kind of our thing. And the other big thing was finally over: last week, we'd both turned in the last of our applications.

"If you knew where we were going, it would ruin my surprise."

I may have protested, but the truth was, I got a thrill from the mystery of it all and I was giddy to have a long night alone with Jag. I could spend forever with all my other senses deprived, just listening to the sound of his voice.

I hadn't dated that many boys in my short life, but every date Jag had ever taken me on rivaled scenes I'd seen in romance movies. Jag's boyfriend game was strong.

"At least tell me which way we're going," I implored.

He laughed, and I loved the sound. "What, like, north, south, east or west? Can you really not wait another half hour to find out?"

"Hmmm," I mused. "Another half an hour...we could be all the way to Red Bluff—that is, unless we're still in Rye and you've just been driving me in circles."

What indeed felt like thirty minutes later, we'd gone from driving on a forest road to the stop-and-go feel of a town. By the time Jag parked, I was itching to stretch my legs and became preoccupied with that once he let me out. It surprised me when he pulled the black satin sleep blinders up from over my eyes. We'd just driven two-plus hours to eat at...

"A pizza place?" I blurted. And not one of those fancy pizza restaurants with table cloths and pizza they had the nerve to charge twice the price for and call flatbread. But I recognized it.

"Wait a minute..." I began, a smile spreading on my face as I swung my gaze to Jag.

"Look familiar?" he asked, with a smile that matched mine. Because this wasn't just any pizza place. It was the pizza place where we'd gone on our first date, when he'd taken me to see the Foo Fighters in Ft. Bragg. This was what required an all-afternoon date and a long drive. Jag was taking us back to this place—back to this night—when we'd had our first kiss.

"Who's playing tonight?" I wanted to know, my mind skipping ahead already, surmising that my suspicions about Jag taking me to a concert had been right.

"You have *got* to learn how to enjoy a good surprise," he came back playfully.

There was something delightful and precious about this trip down memory lane—about recalling how tentative we'd been with one another back then. Jag shocked the hell out of me when he told me that he'd quietly nursed an intense crush on me. He had a good laugh when I revealed that, when we went to the concert together, I hadn't known whether it was a date.

But when we finished our pizza and began the short walk toward the club where we'd seen the Foo Fighters play, there was a suspicious lack of activity around the space. Last time we'd been there, we'd stood in line for a while, so long that Jag had rubbed my shoulders to keep me warm. But tonight—on a Saturday night—there was no line.

"Who did you say was playing again?" I asked, knowing full well that he hadn't. His next words were an obvious dodge.

"I don't think you've heard of the band."

I raised an eyebrow, giving him a look as we were feet away from the door. It wasn't until we were upon it that I saw the sign.

Closed for a private event.

My eyes were wide by the time I looked back at Jag. An expression I couldn't measure had taken over his face. All playfulness was gone from his demeanor.

"Let's see what's inside," he coaxed.

Entering the venue this time was nothing like going in the first, though walking in brought back memories—the old supper-club style seating and the red hues of the decor that were true to the space's name. I remembered the stage and the bandstand, the carpeted stairs, the hard wood parquet dance floor, and the raised booths that fanned out amphitheater style. What was different this time was that the overhead lights were off and the ceiling above the dance floor had been strung with tiny white lights—the most magnificently-arranged white lights I had ever seen.

The tables were illuminated, too, with votives in squat, stained-glass candle holders that diffused the light. All except for one table—the one where Jag and I had sat that night. Our table glowed with the light of what looked like at least twenty small pillar candles on a tiered, modern candelabra.

The craziest thought occurred to me then: was Jag going to propose? We were only eighteen, but I honestly couldn't think of what else would merit a gesture so grand. He'd rented out a popular venue on a Saturday night and it looked like a professional had designed the space. I didn't want to think about how much something like this had cost.

"Jag..." I looked up at him. Suddenly, my favorite leather jacket and my favorite skinny jeans didn't seem like enough for whatever this was. I'd noticed that Jag looked a little more dapper than usual when he picked me up. He'd worn his darker-wash jeans, his pea coat, and—if I wasn't mistaken—he'd used some sort of product in his hair.

"Dance with me?" he asked, regarding me a bit nervously, but extending a steady hand.

I found my voice. "As if I would say no."

An usher who I hadn't seen before came out of nowhere with a flashlight to light our way. We took the steps on the left, which led us to our table. Instead of sitting, we paused there. Jag walked around me to take my jacket. Then he took off his, revealing a fitted black henley I'd never seen him wear.

Time warped a bit then, and my mind played tricks, giving me the strangest sense of déjà vu, only in the wrong direction, where I wasn't seeing the past—I was seeing the future. It didn't feel like I was looking at my teenage boyfriend anymore. It felt like I was standing next to Jagger Monroe, the prodigious, young composer. Jagger Monroe, the man.

God, he's hot.

Even as I was utterly swept away, I couldn't help but to think it—to think about how ensorcelled I still was by him, even after a year. It wasn't the kind of passive admiration all teenage girls had for the finer examples of the male species. There was something specifically and intensely magnetic between me and Jag.

I didn't consciously remember the music go up. Maybe it had been on all along. The downtempo instrumental arrangement of *Times Like These* by the Foo Fighters was the perfect opener. It was a great rendition—mellow and unplugged—just like it had been at the show. Also similar to that night was the fact that Jag had opened with it. It had been the first song of their set when they'd taken the stage a year before.

"Was it exactly a year ago today?" I asked softly as he walked me to the very middle of the space. When we reached our destination, he turned and collected me into his arms, then nodded and smiled as he looked down at me.

"To the day."

I relaxed then, putting my head on his chest and melting into him as we swayed. We were as close as close could be, and still I melted more. It cleansed me and healed me in ways I'd been too scared to admit how badly I needed. I'd been too tightly-wound—too overstressed—for too long a time.

We danced for four songs straight: through *Ain't It the Life*, and *February Stars*, and the best instrumental version of *Hero* I'd ever heard. I basked in the sublime luxury of not having to think. All there was at that moment was me and Jag and the music and not a single thing between us. It was exactly how things were supposed to be.

When *Everlong* came on, I exhaled deeply once again, shedding more emotion than even I realized I'd been carrying. It was the song that had played as we'd shared our first kiss. Apart from this right here—whatever it was—which was easily the best thing that had happened to me all year, that kiss had ranked as the very best moment of my life.

But something was building in Jag—something I could feel thrumming through his body—something that told me again we weren't just here for a walk down memory lane. The past two months had been brutal for both of us. I'd felt for weeks that it had taken a toll on Jag. But I still didn't know what all of this meant.

"There's something I need to say to you..." Jag said finally, a few songs later. He pulled back to look down at me, with more determination than I ever thought I'd seen in his eyes. "There's something I need to show you. Only, it would be wrong—maybe even cruel—to do it more than once. So I'm not gonna harp on it. I'm gonna put it all out there, right now. And the only thing I need from you is a promise that you'll never, ever, *ever* forget this night."

I nodded, not knowing what he would say, but suddenly back on edge. There was something desperate in his voice. I knew instinctively that it had to do with the very foundations of us.

"I don't know where we'll be a year from now, Rox..." I could see it pained him to say it. He paused to let the confession sink in. It was the big, pink elephant in the room—the one who loomed closer the deeper we got into the college thing.

"All I know is, I'm sick of fighting. Even though the whole reason we're coming off as mad at one another is that neither one of us can stand the thought of holding the other one back."

He paused and I swallowed thickly. We'd never used those words to describe the tension between us these past months. Maybe we should have. His hands slid from where they still held me around my waist and reached to grasp my hands.

"I'm not mad at you, Rox," he breathed, his voice cracking a little.

"Me neither," I whispered.

He bent his forehead until it touched mine. Even though we weren't dancing anymore, we swayed a little together.

"And I'm not naïve," he continued. "I know that—if it comes to what I hope it doesn't, we can't have things both ways. I know what being apart from one another probably means."

Tears sprang to my eyes. This was the conversation that we hadn't had. The one we'd needed to. The one it had felt like we couldn't. Of course it had taken something like this—the applications being in and both of us being disarmed in the one place that would cause us to drop our weapons—that found us letting our defenses down.

"But no matter what happens to us in the short-term, and no matter how things seem, I will find my way back to you. And I know how crazy that sounds. I know it sounds like a promise I can't possibly keep. And I don't even need you to believe me. I just need you not to forget how good what we really have is. 'Cause what it's been like lately? That isn't even us."

By then, my first tear had fallen, but Jagger's eyes held only resolve—as if everything hinged on this. It only made me love him more.

"So, promise me, Rox—no matter how things ever look or ever seem—promise me you'll never forget."

9 LANDSLIDE

Oh, mirror in the sky, what is love?
Can the child within my heart rise above?
Can I sail through the changin' ocean tides?
Can I handle the seasons of my life?
Well, I've been 'fraid of changin'
'Cause I've built my life around you.
But time makes you bolder.
Even children get older.
And I'm gettin' older, too.
-Fleetwood Mac, Landslide

ROXY (EARLY MARCH)

Having given up on the illusion that any of us would show up to school, Principal Wyatt had given seniors the day off. It was March 10th—better known as "Decision Day"—the day when colleges that didn't accept on a rolling basis issued undergrad admissions offers.

It was all very high-tech. Beginning at exactly 12PM Eastern Standard Time, students could log onto each school's application portal to learn where and whether they'd gotten in. And so I sat, alone at my kitchen table, phone next to me and laptop open wide, thankful that my dad had acquiesced to my insistence that he go to work. If he were home, it would have only made me more nervous.

My browser was open and I'd launched separate tabs where I'd navigated to each school login screen. Tab by tab, I would go through and learn my fate.

8:49AM PST

With eleven minutes left, I thought back to December, when my dad and I had taken our first father-daughter trip out of state. We'd road tripped on the East Coast looking at schools from the Mid-Atlantic and New England. To my utter terror, I had fallen in love with the top-ranked program: Brown.

There were great schools elsewhere, too. Williams was well-ranked but Williamstown was smaller than Rye—still, it was Massachusetts and a two-hour-away option if Jag ended up in Boston at Berklee. Wellesley was only thirty minutes outside of Boston, and my dad loved the idea of me going to an all-women's school. I'd outright hated Middlebury and had been intimidated by the schools I'd secretly hoped I would adore: Columbia and NYU. I'd applied to all of them anyway. *Just in case*, I thought sardonically. Just in case...I didn't know what.

Just in case I'm too weak not to compromise what's right for me just because I'm in love with a guy who's moving to New York.

I was weak and I knew it, though Jagger did not. I deserved an Oscar for the months of performances I'd put on for him, even after we'd had our heart-to-heart. It was a total mind fuck—loving him too much to let him make the mistake of giving up Juilliard for me and barely loving myself enough not to be on the fence about making the same choice.

8:51

The past few months had been excruciating. Even with Jag and I trying to put the dark days of the fall behind us, our parents' unsolicited advice on the matter had never stopped. Jack and Elsie had tried to appear impartial when they spoke about it, but I could tell they were in favor of Jag going east. My parents had not-at-all tried to appear impartial. As my mother had so tactlessly repeated in recent months, "Don't confuse Mr. Right for Mr. Right Now."

8:54

It didn't help that our friends were still so well-decided on staying together. I'd probed for signs of difficulty, but they still appeared to be sailing through. Declan and Annika had been through some serious shit together, but Zoë and Gunther? Really? She'd once talked about moving to New York to become a fashion designer. But ever since she'd gotten together with Gunther, all she could say was that she'd known since their first kiss that they'd be together forever. I'd kill for her brand of confidence. Sometimes it felt like that with Jagger, but I had to admit: I just didn't know.

8:57

Jagger. I wondered what he was doing at that moment—wondered whether he was alone or flanked by his parents as he waited to learn where he got in. We'd briefly entertained the idea of being together when we found out but decided it might be too much. Suddenly, I wished he was with me right then, no matter what happened.

8:58

The moment of knowing was upon me and I didn't know which outcome I feared most: getting in to Brown, not getting into Brown...each would taste equally bitter. I knew how thankful I should be for the fact that I even had these kinds of choices. Still, it would have been so much simpler if my only options had been one of the UC schools.

8:59

...And, speaking of UC schools, those would be my first stop. It took me a few minutes to get through, no doubt because high school seniors across the country were all logging in at the same time. UCLA had twice the acceptance rate of some of the east coast programs where I'd applied, but it was still hard to get in. Irvine's and UCSB's acceptance rates were twice that of UCLA. Those two would be my safety schools.

I felt eerily detached from myself as I methodically went through and read my results. I'd been most confident about UCSB and Irvine, but when I saw good news from UCLA, I felt a twinge of pride. For someone who'd thought this was the ultimate goal six months before, it didn't feel as good as I knew it should. None of this did. I couldn't stop thinking about Jag.

9:08

Just because I was a glutton for punishment, I chose NYU next, one of the schools I'd liked the least of all. New York just didn't feel like my kind of place. "Congratulations!" the letter began, going on to offer me a spot in the fall class. It felt like a punch in the gut.

9:14

I went to the Columbia web site next. This letter started differently. "We regret to inform you," it began. I trudged on to Williams, then to Wellesley, rejected from the former but not the latter.

9:25

So, New York, L.A. or Boston. Those were my three options so far. If I didn't get into Brown, my choice was still unclear. And I probably wouldn't, I realized. I'd been rejected by the two more prestigious of the schools I'd read the answers to so far and accepted by the ones that were ranked lower.

My heart rate reached unprecedented levels as my phone sounded the familiar chime that rang out any time I received a new text. It sat face down on my table and I was terrified to pick it up. What if it was Jagger? And what would be his news? With a shaking hand, I turned it over. I let out a breath I hadn't known I was holding when I saw it wasn't him. Still, every part of my body tingled with anticipation.

Zoë: *Are you into Brown or what? People are already updating on their results.*

I realized she was talking about Instagram. I thumbed out of my text message window and navigated to the app.

That was when I saw it: my feed was bursting with logos and emblems from various universities and captions announcing success.

@DeckDeckGoose$ had posted the UC Berkeley logo and reported on his feed, *I'm in like Flynn!*

Replying to his thread, *@OhAnnikaOhAnnika$* had written, *I'm packing my bags for Berkeley, too!* Not that we were old enough to drink, but she'd followed it up with the yellow emoji that blew a noisemaker and wore a party hat, then three popped champagne bottles in a row.

@$enorDutton posted that he's *"not doing shit for the rest of the year now that I'm in to Davis".*

@CivilWarBuff$ had posted that he was *"headed south for the winter!"* No surprise there.

@DerbyGirlZoe said she was *"in to Tulane but waitlisted at Duke."*

But I didn't see anything from *@moves_like_jagga.* Not even after I checked. I considered whether to post any of my own news, but immediately decided against it. No offense to Zoë, but I couldn't deal with this right now. When I glanced again at the time, I realized I'd burned a solid few minutes reading other people's news. Results had been out for an eternity and I still didn't know where I stood with Brown.

9:32

Shit. My dad would call soon. Figuring I'd better get it over with, I navigated to the final tab, tapped out my user name and entered my password.

Dear Roxanne,

Congratulations! You have been accepted to Brown University for enrollment in the upcoming fall semester. You have been selected from an extremely competitive applicant group, and are among only 350 students selected specifically for the Literary Arts Program, from a pool of more than 3,500.

In addition to a space in next year's class, we are pleased to be able to name you a Literary Promise Fellow. This prestigious fellowship is awarded to the student who has demonstrated considerable potential in writing, and includes personal mentorship from Literary Arts Program alumni, including National Book Award and Pulitzer Prize winners.

An enrollment packet has been sent to you in the mail and digital versions of these documents can be found on this portal. Please notify our offices directly with news of your intention by April 15th.

On behalf of the faculty and staff at Brown University, we extend our warmest welcome and look forward to seeing you in the fall.

Sincerely,

Grayson Alexander

Director of Admissions

9:45

I didn't even hear him come in; didn't sense him reading over my shoulder; didn't register anything until he was pulling me up and swinging me around in his arms; didn't realize tears were streaming down my face until he pulled away and wiped them from my cheeks; didn't realize until after he'd left that he'd placed a Brown University hat on my head. He'd had faith in me all along.

"I am so proud of you," he whispered, pinning me with intense but watery sage-colored eyes and a sincere but quivering voice.

I cried harder then, understanding for the first time how much Jagger really loved me, how he was still my biggest advocate, how he was truly my best friend. I knew from the second I'd seen his face that he'd gotten into Juilliard, but he'd come in waving his white flag. There'd be no interrogation about whether I got into the New York schools or the Boston ones or any sharing about whether he'd gotten into UCLA. In that moment, he had only pride and congratulations and the most beautiful kind of love.

I should have been indescribably happy. I'd gotten into my dream school and had Jagger's support, no matter my decision. I'd be one of a small handful of people in my extended family to go to college and—for once—my parents agreed about something. In a few short months, I'd be on my own, responsible for nobody but myself. So, why did I feel like leaving Jagger would be the biggest mistake of my life?

10 WHITE FLAG

I know you think that I shouldn't still love you
or tell you that.
But if I didn't say it, well I'd still have felt it.
Where's the sense in that?
I promise I'm not trying to make your life harder
or return to where we were.
I will go down with this ship.
And I won't put my hands up and surrender.
There will be no white flag above my door.
I'm in love and always will be.
-Dido, White Flag

JAGGER (LATE SEPTEMBER)

"Tell me why we're doing this again," I pleaded brokenly.

At that moment, I honestly couldn't remember. How had I ever convinced myself that letting Roxy go like this was remotely acceptable? Parting over something as trivial as the miles between

Providence and Manhattan suddenly seemed like the worst fucking idea ever.

"So we don't end up resenting each other," she whispered just as weakly, her voice as battered and cracked as mine. "So I'm not the reason you gave up Juilliard and you're not the reason I gave up Brown; so that we can do things normal college kids do on weekends instead of spending all our time on trains just to get to one another; so that we don't have to keep saying these awful goodbyes."

Our foreheads were touching. Tears streamed down my face, and I squeezed her more tightly in my arms.

"I should've gone to Berklee—" I swiftly protested.

But we'd had the conversation a thousand times.

"Jagger." She shook her head rapidly. "Berklee would have been a tragedy."

I considered protesting again, but my words fell flat. Nothing I said would change her mind. Never mind that half her resolve came from all the weird baggage she had about not turning out like her mother. I wanted to hate that woman for the multitude of ways her crazy had fucked with Roxy. But what I hated more than anything in that moment was that the rational part of Roxy's resolve was absolutely right about our choice.

What's done is done, and none of that matters now.

All that mattered was standing alone in the middle of Grand Central Station, alone because for as tightly as I held my love in my arms, she was already gone. And in no longer than seven-and-a-half minutes, I wouldn't even have the inadequate comfort of holding her anymore—she'd have walked away to catch her train. And when we met again, even if we were the same, we'd be different.

PART 2

I KEEP FORGETTING (EVERY TIME YOU'RE NEAR)

11 I KEEP FORGETTING

I keep forgettin' we're not in love anymore.
I keep forgettin' things will never be the same
again.
I keep forgettin' how you made that so clear.
I keep forgettin'...
**-Michael McDonald, I Keep Forgetting
(Every Time You're Near)**

ROXY (FRESHMAN YEAR)

My heart shouldn't have been pounding so hard. It was only
10:15 AM, which meant I had another twenty minutes before
Jag was set to show up. Him being there in the flesh would make
my body's reaction understandable at least—his actual proximity
being an appropriate trigger for me to start freaking out.

I was me and Jag was Jag, but even if I wasn't, no boy-loving
girl encountered Jag Monroe without her heart picking up a beat
or ten. If he wasn't even there yet, and I was already jonesing for

him this bad, how the hell was I ever going to survive him and a six hour flight?

Chamomile tea, I said to myself, wishing for something a little harder, but being off campus meant it actually mattered that I was underage. I'd been back to California twice since starting school. The ritual had become jarring—not just leaving the distinct little city of Providence, but going home and seeing my dad and my friends.

"Fucking shit," I muttered aloud the second I hefted my duffel onto my shoulder. It made me immediately regret two things: that I'd stubbornly insisted upon only packing one bag and that, I'd declined the option to check my bag. Maybe it wasn't too late for that plan. Maybe instead of putting all my hopes for not being a blubbering mess when I saw Jagger into a cup of tea, I should go check my bag so I didn't have to worry about looking elegant while carrying this enormous beast.

"You kiss your mother with that dirty mouth?" a smooth voice asked from behind me, nearly making my heart go straight from racing to a complete stop.

I spun around, unable to play it cool for even a second. "Jag?"

His eyes were already sweeping my body from head to toe the way they always did when we hadn't seen one another for a long time. He took his time, as if he were cataloging my features. I liked to do the same thing with him—every time I saw him, he changed. Small changes to anyone else, but not to me. He'd stopped dressings so preppy and had more of a hipster vibe—not full-out hipster, just bolder colors in his wardrobe and garments cut to a closer fit—and a shoe collection had begun to rival mine.

"You just keep getting—" *hotter*. "—taller," I said, managing not to spill my inner monologue, a skill I'd had to work on since our status had reverted to friends. In the halcyon dream of our dating, we'd both become shameless flirts, as if we were making up for lost time spent *not* flirting in the six months it had taken us to get together.

"Either that, or you're slouching under the weight of that bag," he returned with a smirk. "C'mon. Gimme that."

And he plucked the bag I had just struggled to heft on to my shoulders off of my back like it weighed nothing. But he didn't lift it on to his own broad shoulders. He set that, and his own duffel, down on the floor and swept me into an enormous hug.

Hugging Jagger, even if only in greeting, conjured the memory of other embraces—of listening to music on his bed or napping in the hammock in his backyard, safely ensconced in his arms. My nose pressed to his hard muscled chest let me greedily breathe in his distinct scent—one that still recalled Trinity County forests, even though we were miles from home.

And Jag didn't give short hugs, either. He really wrapped himself around me, holding his embrace for a long, long time. It was hard not to tip my head upward like I had done so many times before, to melt under his sage-colored gaze, and to let him pull me in for a kiss.

Just as I was busy trying to be cool, think of something intelligent to say, and *not* pounce on him, the heel of his hand came to my jaw and he threaded his fingers through my hair. I did tip my face up then, not knowing to the marrow of my bones that I would kiss him back if he initiated it.

But in place of the "I still love you. Breaking up was stupid" look I might've been hoping for, I got only his smirk.

"Looks like I won the bet with Declan."

I gave him what must have been a quizzical look.

"He bet me fifty bucks your beanie was surgically-attached to your head."

Being from Southern California and moving to Northern California in high school, I'd been perpetually cold. I'd worn a wide array of knit beanies, daily, to cope. In retrospect, it was laughable. Northern California was like a heatwave compared to the Northeast. Until Providence, I hadn't known the true meaning of cold.

"Looks like I'm not the only one with a new 'do,'" I said, trying to sound normal because Jag's fingers were still in my hair. Hair that I might have spent twice the amount of time styling that morning, but let's not talk about that. On the advice of my room-mate, Jane, I'd kept it long and thanks to an invention called the BaByliss, I could make it fall into soft waves without having any actual hair styling talent.

"Yeah, well, I figured if I'm gonna be a composer, I'd better start looking artsy and brooding." To my utter regret, he removed his hand from my hair long enough to run his fingers through his own. It was longer than I remembered it and he'd either trained it to defy gravity or it held some sort of product.

"Huh," I tutted, cocking my head and pretending to scruti-nize him. "I figured New York just had its hooks in you. Every time I see you, you look less and less west coast."

Jag pretended to pout. "Well, you know, not all of us can look like California girls...."

"No," I agreed, biting my lip to stop a grin that wanted to break through from spreading. *God, it's great to see your face,* I thought to myself, but didn't say. Instead, I finished my thought with, "I suppose not."

He smiled down at me for another long second before angling his head toward the counter. "Come on. Let's check in."

I'd been sitting in the non-secure area, right inside Terminal 8. Instead of heading us toward the automatic kiosks where you could print out a paper boarding pass, Jag went straight to the line with no wait—the one with the small red carpet lining its path—the priority line, because he had it like that.

I hadn't fully appreciated it until we graduated high school—mainly because I hadn't completely known—Jagger Monroe was made of money. In high school, it had felt relative—like his family was just richer than most other families in Rye. Now that we were in the real world, it was abundantly clear that Jag was rich in the absolute sense, rich with a capital "R".

I'd known that his mother had worked in the music business, and that she been some sort of 90s-era producer. What I hadn't known was that Elsie Monroe had co-written a few hit songs. Jag's dad, Jack Monroe, was from old east coast money. He'd shared with me, and me alone, that he'd come into a sizable trust fund when he'd turned eighteen and would come into more when he was twenty-one. It added up to these sorts of things—first-class plane tickets and entry into something called the Flagship Lounge.

At the counter, we chatted intermittently as the exceedingly polite gate agent got Jag's information, checked in his duffel, and, upon his insistence, took mine.

"I get two for free," he'd said. And then my huge bag was gone and it was just me and my purse and Jag with his arm around my shoulders as we sauntered off to security.

This was our little ritual—flying back and forth from home to the East Coast at the same time. It was just like we'd done that first time we'd come in the fall, staying together as long as we could before we had to part ways. For winter and spring breaks, he'd taken the train north and we'd flown back to California out of Logan. That morning, I'd taken an early train so we could both fly out of JFK.

It thrilled and unnerved me in equal measure—how, even though we hadn't seen each other in weeks—ten minutes together found us right back in our rhythm. We chatted and laughed and caught up and smiled all the way through the security line, all the way through stopping at the newsstand to buy gum, all during the time we hung out in Jag's fancy VIP passenger lounge.

I'd been up at the buffet, availing myself of bagel chips and hummus. When I returned to my seat, Jag was holding my magazine.

"Sign this for me?" he asked, reaching into his bag to grab a pen.

Three months before, I'd written a piece for *Entertainment Weekly*—a list of the top ten television theme songs of all time. Since magazines were molasses slow, it had only hit newsstands last week. It was a tiny, half page thing and a list really wasn't the same thing as an article, but for a college kid who had just finished her freshman year, it was a pretty fucking good start.

Heat rose to the tips of my ears, making me aware of my blush, a reaction that only seemed to surface when I was with Jag. I'd expected him to read it online. Hell, I'd sent him the link myself, which he'd apparently sent to his parents, because I'd gotten a nice text from his mom. But Jag had gotten a hard copy, which meant he'd found an actual newsstand to buy it.

"Autographing magazine articles isn't really a thing...you know that, right?" I liked giving him a hard time about his request, even though—secretly—I was brimming with pride.

"Shut up and sign it, Vega. This is gonna be worth something someday. When I tell people I knew the famous Roxy Vega before she became the famous Roxy Vega, I want them to believe me. This'll be my proof."

I plucked the magazine from his hand, not knowing what to write or where to sign. There was barely any room in the margin, so what I wrote was small:

If this ever becomes a collector's item, I'll eat my hat. -Roxy Vega.

He smirked as I handed it back to him and took a quick glance at my words. After replacing it carefully in his messenger bag, he snaked a bagel chip from my plate.

"It was a great piece," he complimented.

I was still getting used to accepting praise for my victories, so I just shrugged. "It was a start."

"Everyone's gotta start somewhere," he argued sensibly.

Focusing on becoming a writer first and a music writer second had been the tradeoff of attending Brown. The small music scene in Providence was no place to break into the business. More often than Jag had visited me there that year, I'd visited him in New York, where the shows were a lot better. Maybe it was because getting to see Jag made me so blissfully happy that it felt New York was growing on me.

Jag was in his element there in a way that surprised me. He'd caught the rhythm and had learned the city and took me to all manner of places. I'd thought that Juilliard might be a little stuffy and intense—full of "serious musicians" with obscure or highbrow tastes. His friends were talented, to be sure—but they were also really nice. When it came to adjusting, he was doing a lot better than me.

That first Christmas home had been the worst, the bliss of having a full two weeks together sullied by the familiarity of places that reminded me how things used to be. It was easier back east, with the distractions of the city, the utter lack of privacy that came with having roommates, and the party-like atmosphere nearly everywhere we went. But back home, when we were all alone, in the quiet surroundings of our forest town, Jagger had no problem sticking to our agreement to just be friends.

I knew it was selfish, but I wanted him to slip—to give me some sign this was as hard for him as it was for me. Even awkwardness would have done, or—even better—putting his foot down like he did in the train station, insisting that us being just friends was horribly, terribly, wrong.

But the moment never came. Jagger was adoring, but platonic; reverent, but respectful; doting, but mindful of boundaries. He still gave amazing hugs that surrounded me with his affection and filled me with his scent, but were no longer followed by kisses.

He still played piano for me, but from new music he had learned, and not a single bar of my song. We still sat in the window seat of his music room, talking until the sun rose, but he now took me home at daybreak instead of letting us snooze in his bed. We still listened to music together, but the upbeat kind—nothing with lyrics that got too deep.

Crueler still was being around Zoë, Gunther, Annika, and Declan. I loved them dearly, but some moments were just too intense. They were all kind enough to be sensitive—to not flaunt how well things were turning out for them. They were all happily un-broken-up.

Before arriving back to Providence from break, I had dreaded another excruciating goodbye—imagined Grand Central all over again, but in the far less romantic environs of Logan Airport. There were no tears this time—not ones that I let shed until I was on the train, listening to the single song he'd sent me minutes after we'd parted. It was *Ordinary World*, by Duran Duran. The lyrics were hopeful, but it had felt like goodbye.

"Don't be mad," Jag whispered in my ear as we approached gate C35. It was time for us to board the plane. I'd heard him ask the counter attendant whether we could get seats together, which she'd confirmed, and I was just about to refresh my boarding pass on my phone.

"Mad about what?" I asked distractedly, pausing where many passengers were already standing, waiting for their group to be called. But Jag pulled me forward, walking me toward where only three or four people were boarding the plane.

"I got you an upgrade," he said.

My eyes widened. "Jag—" but he cut me off.

"This calls for celebration, don't you think?"

He plucked my phone out of my hand, continued navigating

to my digital wallet and pulled out my boarding pass. He refreshed the screen and handed it back over. My eyes snapped to the screen. Sure enough, it said I was in seat 2C.

Still gob smacked, I followed him blindly, scanning my QR code at the terminal, then following him down the jet way, then into a leather seat bigger than my dad's recliner back home. The flight attendant was already serving the others from a full tray of champagne in stemless glasses. I was guessing that when you paid ten times the amount for a plane ticket, no one cared if you weren't twenty-one. Jagger accepted on both of our behalf.

"So what are we celebrating?" I asked absently, still inspecting my luxurious seat. I, for one, was celebrating not having to sardine myself in a coach seat for the next six hours.

"Surviving a year we weren't sure we could survive."

My hands halted on the recliner controls and my gaze snapped up to Jag. His eyes were as somber as his voice. Last year, neither of us had been able to shut up about it. This year, neither of us had talked about it out loud.

"It doesn't feel like something to celebrate," I choked out, my voice suddenly and suspiciously quiet, and on the verge of breaking.

"It was better than the alternative." But he didn't sound convinced. "Now we've been in it. We know it for sure. The long distance thing never would have worked."

Going to UCLA together would have. I thought but didn't say. If we'd gone there, maybe we'd be winding our way up the Pacific Coast Highway in his Tiguan, en route to Trinity County, right now.

"To sacrifices..." he toasted, lifting his glass and looking at me intensely—the way he'd looked at me on only one other night. "...giving up what you can't have now, and waiting for things to be set right in the end."

12 I'M NOT IN LOVE

I'm not in love, so don't forget it.
It's just a silly phase I'm going through.
And just because I call you up,
don't get me wrong. Don't think you've got
    it made
I'm not in love, no, no...it's because.
-10cc, I'm Not in Love

JAGGER (SOPHOMORE YEAR)

It was 8:20 PM; I was ten minutes early for my rendezvous
with Roxy on Skype. I'd eaten dinner, triple-checked my appear-
ance, poured myself a drink, and bribed my roommate to stay the
hell out. The carefully-selected playlist hummed at an acceptable
volume in the background—I wondered whether Roxy would
pick up on its clues.

I smirked when I caught an eyeful of myself in the reflection
of the window. Roxy was going to love my costume. We had an

8:30 date to play a little game: guess which rock icon I am for Halloween? And, when I say "date", I mean totally platonic appointment that will be the highlight of my week with a woman who is, technically, my friend.

Don't feel sorry for me. Whenever I start wishing we were more, I remind myself of last year. I deserved a Tony for my theatrics at Christmas when I pretended I was handling things just fine. That trip took so much out of me that when I returned to New York, I was catatonic for days. I holed up in my apartment, drinking too much, eating too little and not answering my phone, straight from New Years to Martin Luther King.

Those were dark times, last winter. I'd pulled away from her then, as much as I could without having her see through how it pained me to keep her in my life. That all changed the Thursday night she called me, near tears, after some creepy dude had followed her home from a party. Her roommate was away for the weekend, so she was scared and home alone. Don't think I didn't borrow a car and make it to Providence before dawn because I certainly fucking did.

It was the longest drive of my life, forget that I drove so fast I shaved an hour off the time. It had taken about five seconds of hearing her voice on that call before I snapped out of my months-long daze and got some fucking perspective. Roxy was alone, in a strange city, keeping company with people she'd just met, half of who were horny little pricks who would try to fuck her. It wasn't like in Rye, where all the boys knew that me or her father would crush them if they looked at her the wrong way.

She was so strong and independent—so much larger than life to me that sometimes I forgot she was just a girl, a girl who called because she needed her best friend. And, thank God she did. Thank God she called me even though I'd been acting weird for months. But, all of that was over. I knew I would never let my feelings for her put me in a position to fail her again.

That weekend changed things—set things right between us—
as right as they could be. For the first time in months, I held her
without worrying whether my embrace was too close. For the first
time in months, I slept with my arms around her in bed. Nothing
happened—nothing even came close— though I felt the current of
attraction, strong as ever, between us.

By the end of the weekend, after I'd dragged her around Providence buying her a pocket Taser, a pepper spray keychain, a cute
little flask so she wouldn't have to take any strange drinks, and
enrolling her in the best self-defense class in the city, it became
clear what had changed. Eight months of college had taught us
the same lesson: this new lifestyle was rich with acquaintances
but almost bankrupt of friends. And we couldn't throw that away
—couldn't let wanting something we couldn't have get in the way
of us taking care of each other.

So I focused on carving her out a new, unnamed place in my
life, and on being the best friend that I could. When I got back to
New York that Sunday night, I'd gotten my recording equipment
out and headed straight for my piano. Ignoring my homework, I'd
made her a recording of *Wicked Little Town* and sent her a
recording. My phone had chimed just as I was getting into bed—
she'd sent me a song on, too. I 'd let it lull me to sleep. It was
Cyndi Lauper's *Time After Time*.

My Skype phone chimed, jarring me from my memories—
Roxy was trying to video call me. Rather eagerly, I picked up. I
smiled as her video image came up on my screen. In response, she
burst out laughing.

"Ziggy Stardust?" she laughed. "Technically, not a rock star,
but whatever—your costume is epic! Who did your lightning
bolt?"

I grinned, thrilled that my costume had earned her approval,
and also because I loved seeing her smile and hearing her laugh.
Even with the eye makeup and crazy wig she was wearing

concealing her natural beauty, my girl was still absolutely gorgeous.

"Eric," I admitted, referring to my roommate. "And I believe we said rock *icon*, not rock star."

"Fair enough," she agreed, still chuckling a little.

"So, who are you?" I asked, already knowing the answer, a cheap ploy to make her get up and turn around. She backed her desk chair up a few feet so I could get a better look.

"Uh-uh..." I tutted. "I need the full effect."

She rolled her eyes, but took the bait. When she got up, I saw that she was wearing the tightest, sexiest leather pants I had ever seen.

I was instantly hard, as would be any other man who saw her tonight. She'd gained two-thirds of the freshman fifteen, supplying her nicely with a few more curves. Stuff those curves into some kick-ass pants, high-heeled shoes, and Joan Jett's requisite scowl, and men would be lining up to get a piece. I did not want her going out like that.

"Seriously? You don't know yet?" she asked in disbelief, taking her seat back at her desk. "And, don't even try to get me to sing you a clue."

I liked the thought. "Come on, just a few lines," I begged.

She stuck out her tongue.

"Very mature, *Joan Jett...*" I retorted with emphasis.

She put her tongue back in her mouth and her hand disappeared from view momentarily—long enough for her to lift her cup. She tipped it at me and I raised my own.

"What are we drinking to?" I asked, still smiling.

"To all of the rock and roll greats."

We settled into a conversation then, talking about everything and nothing, from how school was going, to politics, to friends. Her father had gotten back together with Sadie the nurse—Roxy thought it was getting serious; Zoë was doing costume design for some big-deal Civil War reenactment thing she and Gunther were a part of; Annika had done a one-eighty on going pre-law and switched her major to gender studies; Roxy planned on submitting an essay to a literary magazine.

Whenever we talked, I looked for clues as to how she was doing. Did she look healthy? Was she getting enough sleep? Would she give it to me straight, or would her voice betray her eyes? Did she really like it there? Was she happy? If she was, was it because of a guy? Our don't ask, don't tell policy on dating never stopped me from wondering what might be going on.

"You know those pants'll have every guy in the place all up in your shit," I remarked when I knew our conversation was close to its end. Her creepy roommate Jane had breezed in moments before, saying something to Roxy, and interrupting our perfectly good time. "Please tell me you're not going to this thing alone," I begged, silently hoping that any planned chaperone was not a guy.

"Didn't you see Jane's costume?" Roxy asked, craning her neck to see where her roommate had gone. "She's going as Cherie Curry."

No sooner had the words exited her mouth than did a drunk-looking Jane land in Roxy's lap and plant a kiss at the corner of Roxy's mouth. Jane looked right at me, into the camera.

"They were hooking up, you know."

God, her eyes were scary.

"Erm..."

Roxy pushed Jane off her lap and looked at me apologetically. "I think I gotta go."

"I'm not kidding, Rox." I said in a voice that was trying for threatening but that came out as more of a plea.

She knew what I meant. *Don't let any guys get fresh with you.*

"Jagger, thanks to you I'm a green belt in Tae Kwon Do," she pointed out with more than a hint of compassion. "And, I am Luke Vega's daughter."

I lowered my voice. "Roxy, what you are is smoking hot, and some drunken moron won't see far enough past your ass to care whose daughter you are."

She blushed as if I'd paid her a compliment and not stated a simple fact.

"You know I only worry because I care about you, Rox. I just want you to be safe."

She smiled a little and whispered, "I know."

It was moments like this—moments when I could practically feel her—that I wanted to have last forever.

"You be careful, too. You rock that Bowie the right way and it won't just be the girls after *your* sexy ass—so watch out for those boys."

I chuckled. "I will."

"Roxy, come *on!*" shouted Jane's voice from somewhere off camera. I suddenly hated that crazy woman.

"Good night, Jag."

Her eyes were soft as she said it.

"Good night, love."

Yeah, sometimes, I slip.

13 SILVER SPRING

Time cast a spell on you
but you won't forget me.
I know I could have loved you
but you would not let me.
I'll follow you down until the sound
of my voice will haunt you.
You'll never get away from the sound
of the woman that loved you.
-Fleetwood Mac, Silver Spring

ROXY (JUNIOR YEAR)

"I think that's his train," I muttered biting my nails in anticipation, trying not to bounce in my seat at the outdoor café.

I looked to Jane hopefully. She rolled her eyes before pulling out a Camel Light.

"We're not in Switzerland, Rox. We'll probably be here another hour. These Spanish trains take their goddamn time."

She lit her cigarette and inhaled deeply. I sipped my sangria in defeat. We were at the train station in Donostia, better known as San Sebastián, waiting for Jagger and his friend. I was starting to get antsy—his train was already forty-five minutes late, and we'd be together for fewer than thirty-six hours.

I'd been in San Sebastián for the first part the summer doing research for a professor writing about terrorism paradigms world-wide. I was charged with deconstructing the role of ETA and other Basque separatist efforts in the corresponding regions in France and Spain. My primary contact was my Brown professor's colleague at the University of the Basque Country. In that short time, I'd already fallen in love with Spain, and my Spanish was improving.

My six-week assignment had ended the week before, and it was already the first week in July. I spent a few days exploring the coast with Beatriz, a friend I'd met two weeks after arriving in Donostia. Beatriz and I had returned on Saturday, just in time for me to meet up with Jane. In the two days since, we'd been catching up and I'd been not-so-patiently waiting for Jagger.

Contrary to Jane's initial cynicism, it was—indeed—a train. What seemed like far too many people got off. I tried not to seem overly-eager as I scanned the crowd and didn't see a trace of Jagger. I didn't want to think about how disappointed I would be if something had happened and he hadn't gotten off.

"Kaixo, preciosa," said a smooth voice behind me before strong arms pulled me up and into a tight hug.

I inhaled his scent and sighed contentedly. Trust Jagger to know how to greet me flawlessly in Basque.

"Kaixo, querido," I murmured into his ear, every cell in my body overcome with relief.

We hugged for a long time. He smelled wonderful for someone who'd been on an all-night train and his arms around me felt predictably amazing. I made no effort to pull away, but when we finally did, he cradled my jaw in his palms. I got a good look at him then. It no longer surprised me that he only got better-looking with time.

"Cato, this is Roxy," he said, not taking his eyes off of mine.

Oh, that's right—we're not alone.

Remembering my manners, I stepped forward to greet Cato with four very European kisses on the cheek. Jagger, ever the gentleman, did the same with Jane, though I happened to know she kind of freaked him out.

She was definitely weird, but somehow, Jane had become one of my best friends. We were planning to get an apartment together during our last year at Brown, as we'd both be gone Junior year due to study abroad. We'd spend the next three weeks touring Northern Europe until we parted ways in Paris. I'd spend two weeks there with Zoë until heading to Scotland. My study abroad was at the University of Edinburgh.

Jagger, meanwhile, was doing a semester in Vienna at yet another impossible-to-get-into program for musical prodigies. Determined to hit all the best summer festivals, he'd insisted we meet in Pamplona for the Running of the Bulls before he and Cato headed south to some concert in Morocco. We had tentative plans to meet up again for Oktoberfest, but if that didn't fly, this would be it until Christmas.

By nightfall, my face hurt from laughing so much—such was always my time with Jagger. The country I had already come to love became one more magical with him. That first night was a late one. We'd driven together to Pamplona and immediately joined in on the festivities. The carefree spirit of the Spanish was contagious, and we'd eaten well, drunk better, and made new friends.

I awoke in his arms, in his small single room in our hotel, to the sounds of people already gathered on the streets. We lay in easy silence, smiling into each other's eyes. He kissed my nose and informed me that I still talked in my sleep. Coaxed out of bed by Jane's ribbing ("Dry your dick off and get dressed!" she had cried. "It's starting in half an hour."), we got up. Jagger needed no such grooming, as we'd simply enjoyed a fully clothed slumber in one another's embrace.

"Today's gonna be great," he whispered in my ear, holding me protectively in a recessed doorway once we finally made it to the street.

And, it was. I nearly peed my pants at least twice, once from laughing at Jagger's commentary on the spectacle of brave men charging ahead of the enormous beasts, and again at one point when said beasts got too close to our hiding place for comfort.

We napped again in the afternoon, enjoyed an amazing dinner at an outdoor café, and drank in a cellar bar for a while with Cato and Jane. The two had taken a strange liking to one another and, at eleven at night, informed us that they'd be spending the rest of the evening alone.

So we walked. It felt like we walked the entire city. It seemed like we talked of every subject under the moon. Under the moon was where we found ourselves at some lookout above the city, watching the landscape sprawled out below.

I was telling him about one of my professors, a Pulitzer Prize winner who was a literary genius but who took himself way too seriously, when I stopped mid-story as soon as I noticed a strange smile ghosting over Jagger's lips.

"What?", I asked, cocking my head, unable not to smile, myself. Jagger Monroe turned me into a goofy, grinning idiot and I couldn't find it in myself to care.

He shook his head slightly, insisting, "Nothing. I'm listening."

I kicked his foot a little.

"No, you're smiling. Now, tell me what."

He looked down for a minute, worrying a pebble between

agile toes, let his eyes scan the horizon for a long moment before they came back to me.

"You're happy, Roxy."

His lashes fluttered slightly as he said it, his smile faltering for a split second as sorrow clouded his eyes.

Oh, Jag.

"Today I'm happy," I corrected gently, laying my head on his shoulder. "Every other day I'm just content."

Maybe it was the wine; in that moment I couldn't think of a single reason to pretend he didn't still sit near the center of my world. The decision of a naïve, eighteen-year-old me had done nothing to change how I felt about Jagger; and twenty-year-old me had nothing to prove.

"C'mere."

His whispered command was more like a plea, and he didn't wait for my response before bringing me into his fold. Instead of remaining side-by-side facing the vista, he encircled me in his arms with me between his legs, my back to his front. And, just like that, we were silent, our stories forgotten like the wine—now untouched—by our side.

Time warped. We may have heard the sounds of the celebrating city below us for hours. The stars in the night sky seemed to take forever to fade. My eyes were closed when the sun peeked over the horizon.

I melted into him. He held me tighter. I listened to him breathe. He planted soft kisses in my hair, and I couldn't be sure but I think he might have whispered my name. He cupped my jaw just as I felt the warmth of sun, the tip of his nose tracing the line of mine before sweeping me in for a kiss.

I still love you, it hummed. *I never stopped loving you. I'm not sure I ever will.*

It was the epitome of decadence—both sinful and sweet. His tongue, as wickedly skilled as ever, stroked mine deliciously, fanning the flame that had never stopped burning inside. Yet, his lips—so gentle and deliberate—calmed me, their softness a salve to my soul.

"Roxy," I heard him whisper, this time certain that he'd said my name. I looked, and his eyes were aflame with sunrise. He hesitated to speak, but my mouth silenced his, eager once again to taste home.

Both of us knew by then: the confession would change nothing between us, just as not confessing hadn't made any feelings go away. We both had lives to get back to. It seemed we'd passed through yet another gate on this bittersweet journey: being as tethered to one another as ever, but without the strings.

Later, at the train station in Donostia, he bought me breakfast at the same café where he'd found me two days before. Jane and Cato conversed with their voices; Jagger and I, with our eyes.

Take care of yourself. You know I worry.

Jagger spread jelly on his croissant, keeping half for himself and passing half to me.

Don't let those prima donnas in Vienna get to you.

I replaced his hand with my own as it tugged through his crazy hair.

I'll miss you, too.

His thumb gently tugged my bottom lip from where my teeth worried it.

I know. We'll see each other soon.

After we'd finished eating, he fiddled with my phone for twenty minutes with his right hand as his left held mine atop my knee. I didn't see the entire playlist he was making, but smiled sadly when I caught a glimpse of *Midnight Radio*.

Walking to the platform, we trailed Jane and Cato, going slowly, hand in hand. And then we stopped. And he turned to me, looking down into my eyes.

This was always the hardest moment—the moment of good-bye, though we rarely, if ever used that word anymore.

"Those Scottish guys are naked under their kilts—you know that, right?"

My sad smile mirrored his own.

"You have more talent in this little finger...", I choked out holding up my right pinkie.

I trailed off before my voice *really* caught.

He kissed my finger, and left.

14 WHAT HURTS THE MOST

What hurts the most was being so close,
and havin' so much to say,
and watchin' you walk away.
And never knowin' what could've been.
And not seein' that lovin' you
is what I was trying to do
-Rascall Flats, What Hurts the Most

JAGGER (SENIOR YEAR)

"Thanks for saving me a seat, Mr. Vega," I said breathlessly after making my way to the chair he'd directed me to by text, minutes before Roxy's graduation was set to begin. I'd just seen my own parents off to the airport that morning and helped my roommate pack up his stuff the day before. I still had half a week's worth of my own packing to do, but already, I had one foot out of New York.

"Good to see you, kid."

To my utter surprise, Luke Vega rose and greeted me with a cheerful smile, gave me a man hug and held me for a minute by the shoulders at arm's length, getting a good look at me before I sat down.

"You're looking well, Mr. Vega," I managed.

And a lot friendlier than you used to be.

"None of that Mr. Vega shit. You're not in high school anymore. Call me Luke."

His smile soured a bit as he looked toward the person in the seat on the other side of me, who I hadn't yet heeded given Luke's hearty hello.

"You remember Roxy's mother..."

I turned to Star Vega, who had always had us on a first name basis. "Of course," I said with a polite smile and a lean over to kiss her cheek. "It's lovely to see you, Star."

Apart from my own high school graduation, I hadn't ever seen Star and Luke Vega together. Roxy still didn't have much contact with Star, and had some trepidation about her mother even attending her graduation. I'd already resolved to distract Star some, and to diffuse things between her parents, if it would make things easier on Roxy.

But that wasn't going to be an issue—at least not yet. Luke was too busy grilling me about what my plans were and hearing about my final year at Juilliard. He knew an astonishing set of specifics around what I had done, which meant he'd either googled me or that Roxy brought me up in conversation. A lot.

"You ever meet this Poindexter kid?" Luke asked out of the blue. People in caps and gowns were lining up and I'd become distracted scanning the crowd for Roxy. Luke's mention of her boyfriend snapped my attention right back.

"I think his name's Percival," I pointed out mildly. Star looked up from her phone.

"Luke knows his name. He just doesn't like him."

"What do you think of him?" Luke wanted to know, leaning forward a bit in his seat. I was pretty sure Luke hated him, and my baser instincts told me to pile on. The truth was, this Percival guy was nowhere near good enough for Roxy.

"I hear he's a talented writer," I hedged. But Luke scoffed.

"Every blowhard nowadays thinks he's gonna write the great American novel."

"And I think he just won some prestigious award," I continued.

"Come on, get to it..." Luke insisted. "Do you like this kid or not?"

I didn't totally want to sell the guy out. After all, I'd been in his position before—subject to the harsh, scrutinous eye of Luke Vega. But I didn't want to bless him either, which would run counter to my own self-interests.

"I trust Roxy's judgment, and I'm sure there's something great she sees in him, but..." I paused for effect. "He listens to Nickelback. In a non-ironic way. And I heard him say to Roxy once, and I quote: "David Bowie is overrated"."

There were plenty of lackluster things I could find to say about Percy. I might have chosen that one knowing that Bowie was one of Luke's favorite artists. But that was neither here nor there. When Luke seemed deeply scandalized, I knew my comment had hit its mark.

The ceremony itself was unexciting. The university president's speech was dry, but I couldn't blame Luke for being rapt with attention. This was surely a day he had imagined for years. Since I'd heard plenty of inspirational words at my own graduation, I scanned to look for Roxy in the crowd. When I followed Star's stare to see whether she'd done the same, I actually found Roxy. A warmth spread in my chest and a smile pulled at my lips, even from this far.

"I misjudged you," Star said out of the blue. I swung my gaze over to her, not having expected much in the way of conversation. She'd barely said two sentences since I'd sat down.

"I misjudged Roxy, too." Star shifted her gaze back to her daughter. "She's made better choices than I have. And she's always been a better judge of character..." Star said it slowly, settling her gaze on me once more. "Roxy will make the right choice in the end."

I was confused for a second, and then it clicked: she was talking about Percy. It picked at scabs I'd been desperate to heal. Not about Percy—about Roxy and me in general. I knew she was too smart to end up with a guy like him, but I did worry about her meeting a much better guy.

By my math, the probability of this was only getting bigger. Without a punishing course load, she would have more time to date. Providence was a small city, so not a lot of fish, but Roxy was already on her way to a bigger pond. And our stars continued to misalign.

I could have brushed it off, or just nodded, or discredited Star Vega completely. She might be dead wrong about Roxy to the extent that they weren't close, but I sensed motherly wisdom at play. So I said what I was thinking, and did it with a little shrug. "Roxy has a lot of options. She can have whoever she wants."

Star smiled in a way that reminded me of Roxy and her eyes flickered—for only a split second—to Luke. "When it's the right person, you never stop looking for a second chance."

Two hours later, graduation was over and we were at a crowded restaurant with an outdoor garden bar that doubled as a waiting area. They were running late with our reservation, so Roxy and I were killing time and taking a break from her parents.

Star had said she had a phone call to make. Luke had said he wanted to stretch his legs, which left Roxy and I alone for the first time that day. I'd showered her with congratulatory hugs earlier, and had her dad take a picture of us with her holding up her degree. But now that it was just us, my arm was around her again.

"I wish I could've come to yours," she said with an apology in her eyes. It was a warm day and we'd each ordered a beer. We found an empty little rope swing bench at the far end of the garden under a big, old tree.

I waved my hand and brushed it off. "You had finals."

"Still..." She looked past my shoulder and collected her words. "This moment is..." she let out a breath, then looked back over at me. "...why we did it, you know? So that you'd have Juilliard and I'd have this."

I was dying to ask her. I couldn't spit out the question I'd never stopped asking myself: had we made the right decision? Were we actually better off? I wasn't sure that I was. At twenty-two, I was accomplished. But I still went to bed alone.

"You made it to all of my performances," I pointed out, resisting the urge to tuck her hair behind her ear. "In my business the performances are more important than the graduation. Trust me—it was boring as hell."

She rolled her eyes. "Yeah. I'm sure sitting through a thousand names being called is exactly how you wanted to spend a beautiful Saturday afternoon in June."

A lump formed in my throat. "I'd have sat a lot longer, just to hear yours."

But I didn't want today to turn into one of those kinds of days. I wanted today to be happy. So instead of mentioning my immeasurable pride again, I made light.

"Besides, I wasn't bored while they were calling the other nine-hundred-ninety-nine names. I got to sit next to your mother."

She cringed and put her hand over her lovely face. "Holy hell. I'm sorry."

"You know, I think she's getting better in her old age."

Roxy gave me a look. "She's not even forty. You know that, right?"

"Your dad likes me a lot better now, too..." I baited.

She kept her eyes on me as she took a sip of her beer. "Yeah, tell me about it."

I chuckled again, surprised by her reaction. I'd thought news of her father's favor would surprise her too. "Alright...what does that mean?"

"You've become, like, this God-like figure to him. He hates every guy I date. Which is pretty easy, 'cause he compares them all to you."

"Oh, yeah?"

The exact moment I realized that my tone had gone high and delighted, Roxy said, "Try not to sound so impressed with yourself."

I made a mental note to have a beer with Luke Vega later, content to know that we had more in common than a simple dislike of just-this-latest-guy. Maybe Luke really was in my corner. Could he be gunning for me? Had he been gunning for me all along?

"And what will Percival be doing with *his* degree?" I asked.

She smiled a little even from beneath her warning look. "I swear to God, Jag—you've got to stop calling him that to his face. It really irritates him, okay?"

"So I'll be seeing him again?" I asked, after I'd held my hands up in silent surrender and promised telepathically to honor her request. It would take effort, but, for Roxy, I'd refrain from being a dick.

She didn't look disappointed when she said, "Probably not."

Oh, thank fuck, I breathed to myself in relief, then had the impulse to tell Luke. Seeing his daughter graduate from Brown and hearing she was breaking up with someone unworthy of her sounded like a perfect day.

"He's moving to Lhasa for six months to live in a Buddhist monastery. He needs to cleanse his spirit in order to release his writing muse."

I did my best to button it down, biting my lip as I struggled to keep a straight face.

"It's okay...you can laugh." Roxy raised her hand in the air in front of her, making small circles with her finger in a gestured that told me to go on.

"I'm sure he's very talented," I said, managing not to chuckle at that very moment, though the smile I allowed might have held the hint of a snicker.

"You wouldn't know it to look at him, but he really kind of is." She said it in that honest way of hers, not to push my buttons, but it still made me a little jealous.

"You two gonna stay in touch?" I couldn't not ask.

"Casually." She shrugged. "But we're done with dating."

Of late, I'd also had to entertain a frightening thought: in the irony of ironies, Roxy was set to move in to my New York apartment. I'd gone in with my parents on buying a place when I'd first gone to Juilliard, but had gotten a roommate so I could have the college experience. The long term-plan was for me to live there indefinitely and for my family to keep it as a pied-à-terre. I'd always known one day I'd move back to California, but working in the music industry, I would never not have ties to New York.

But off I was to L.A. to intern with an Oscar-winning composer on an epic fantasy film trilogy. The thing was, I'd only looked for jobs in L.A. Because I thought Roxy might end up there, too. It had been delicate—trying to broker us ending up in the same city without us actively being in a relationship. Deciding to move somewhere together would have been much easier if we were.

But Roxy and I weren't dating. And, at the time we were looking for jobs, I couldn't even bring up the possibility of getting back together. It had felt funny to even hint at it, seeing as how both of us had been dating other people. Roxy knew some part of me would always be in love with her, and I knew the reverse was true. What she didn't know was how getting us back together was still at the forefront of my mind.

For a minute—actually, for a month—it had looked like it might work out. Roxy had offers in-hand for a few staff writer positions in L.A. She'd never stopped saying that her endgame was to live on the West Coast. Then she'd gotten a call from Carson Jaye, a big rock star biographer who had followed some of her writing. Believing in her talent, she'd offered Roxy an apprenticeship. Now, instead of writing in L.A., Roxy would travel the world, shadowing her and the rock stars she was profiling, and being based—just like Carson—in New York.

The pay was predictably paltry, which was where my offer of an apartment had come in. I wasn't using it and even if I were, I'd have insisted she stay. My place was big. It was furnished. It was in an extremely safe neighborhood and, best of all for Roxy, it was free. Everything about it was perfect—except we'd missed our chance. Again.

15 THE CATERPILLAR

You flicker
And you're beautiful
You glow inside my head
You hold me hypnotized
I'm mesmerized
Your flames
The flames that kiss me dead
-The Cure, The Caterpillar

ROXY (ONE YEAR **Later)**

"You're drunk," Jagger accused with entirely too much joy, his eyes alight with humor, saying the word in a way that drew out the "r".

He moved his feet from where they rested on the lower rungs of my bar stool long enough to let me climb back on. I'd just returned from my second trip to the ladies' room and the place was emptying out—getting quieter the later into the night it got.

"That's what happens when you put a twenty-dollar-bill in the jukebox an hour and a half ago and it still hasn't played your songs," I retorted, grabbing a peanut.

But Jag just smirked. "Actually, that's what happens when you drink three sidecars and Joe's pouring."

Jag jutted his head toward the space in front of me. It seemed that, while I was gone, Joe had poured me number four. The man had been bartending at Googie's since Jagger's college days. The place was on Sullivan Street, around the corner from all the bars on Bleecker that had live music. It was Saturday night and Jag and I had just been to see a band.

"Why aren't you drunk?" I asked, narrowing my own eyes as I crushed the peanut shell in my fingers and let it fall into my hands.

"Easy..." Jag's smile widened and he held his own newly-filled highball glass up in silent toast before taking a drink. "This is just seltzer with lime. I pay Joe to water it down."

"Shut up," I admonished, giving his knee a little slap a second before I snatched his glass from his hand. It was full enough that it spilled a little. My eyes stayed on his as I brought it to my lips, and he half-laughed while licking clear liquid off of the heel of his hand. Clear liquid that turned out to be a gin and tonic so strong, it made me sputter. That was all it took for Jag's half-laughter to turn to full laughter.

I threw him an apparently un-menacing glare as I handed him back his glass. He took a healthy sip before putting it down.

"Not all of us can be 6'2" and a hundred-seventy-five pounds of pure muscle," I muttered petulantly. He had a clear advantage. I was barely a buck thirty-five.

"Oh, you like this, do you?" He put on a sultry voice and brought his hand to his midsection, running his fingers up and down. Even through his shirt, I could see the faint ripple of his abs.

"I plead the fifth." I popped a peanut in my mouth, looked down the bar and feigned disinterest. My gaze snapped back to him when I felt the barstool beneath me pull forward in a quick slide. His feet were on the rungs again and the stools were as close together as our tangle of limbs would allow. Jag had reversed his feet and pulled me in by my toes.

"But you're so honest when you're drunk," he said with a little pout.

"And you're so flirty," I came back, not too drunk to speak the truth.

He shrugged as he shucked a peanut of his own, cracking it at the seam with two agile fingers. "Don't blame me. You're the one who's hot."

And, there he is.

Not that I was going to complain about flirtatious Jag. Something about the two of us now was easy—like things we'd been careful of once upon a time, we'd gotten over. When flirtatious Jag was gone again, I would overthink whether the way we'd been this time was a good or bad omen for our long-term prospects. For now, I would enjoy how close he was sitting, and the too-delicious scent of his more-chiseled-every-time-I-saw-him-body.

"I dunno..." I said lightly. "You're the one who's been working out."

His gaze stayed on me as he gave me a cheeky smile. "So you *do* like it..."

I just shrugged and picked up another peanut.

"Does *Dan* work out?" Apart from his smile, Jag's eyes now held a wicked glint.

"You're never gonna let me live that down, are you?" I groaned.

Jag shelled a peanut of his own and grinned like the Cheshire cat. "Nope."

Jag had been in town for a week already, in from L.A. for

some sound mixing workshop that sounded technical as hell and that had taken up most of his time. It was just as well. I'd been on deadline for two freelance articles and I owed my boss, Carson, pages for a memoir we were ghosting.

My apartment was Jag's apartment so, of course, he was staying with me. Two days earlier, he'd walked in on me and our neighbor, Dan, in the mail room. Jag was a minute behind me, shooting the shit with the doormen. By the time he caught up to me so we could take the elevator up to the apartment together, there was Dan, trying to ask me out. Again.

"You gotta give the guy credit for trying." I swayed a little in my seat.

Jag laughed heartily. "I do? That guy was old enough to drink before we were born. I've never been so embarrassed watching a guy trying to pick up a woman in my life. You'd think he'd have learned some game in all that time..."

"Some women might consider him to be a silver fox..." I baited, just to mess with Jag.

The hallmark of Dan's look was his swish of black-gray hair that was arranged in a stylish pouf tendril on top of his head, and his impeccably-groomed, medium-cropped silver beard. Jag was probably right—Dan was probably around twice their age, but fifty was a stretch. His face was somewhat youthful and I'd always guessed he'd simply gone gray prematurely.

"I'll bet he was hot shit back in his day..." I continued.

"And when would that have been? 1968?"

"'68 was a good year. That's the year Simon & Garfunkel released *Mrs. Robinson*."

Jag blinked, then said, indignantly, "Yeah. On the soundtrack to *The Graduate*—a movie about an inappropriate relationship between a parental figure and an innocent young man."

I giggled. Jag was funny and not many people could make me laugh like this. Definitely no one in New York.

"You should be thanking me, Rox..." He shelled another peanut. "Friends don't let friends date men who groom their beards in public, and, before you ask—yes, I've seen him on the street corner whipping out his comb."

Even Jag himself couldn't keep a straight face as he reported this egregious little morsel. I swayed in my seat again. I was definitely on my way to being drunk. I took sweeping breaths in order to slow down my laughter.

"Well, you saw for yourself. Me and Dan are *not* gonna become a thing. And even if I didn't have the situation under control—*which I totally did*," I said with emphasis, "you going all papa bear pretty much cinched it."

Jag bit his tongue against anything he might have said at that moment, but didn't look repentant. "Papa bear" was kinder than the more accurate term.

Jag had all but pissed on me when he'd walked into the room, throwing out a, "Hey, man...long time, no see". He'd halted at my side and thrown a hand over my shoulder while "catching up" with Dan. It had thrown Dan totally for a loop to see that the former and current tenants of 10C seemed to know one another —maybe *like that*.

And the message Jag's eyes telegraphed was loud and clear:

Hey, man... How you been? Yeah, that's right. I'm still in the picture. The girl in 10C isn't just some hot, young thing. You're twice her age, you perv. So stay the hell away from her. Capisce?

"So what does it take to impress a woman like Roxy Vega these days?" Jag changed the subject and turned on the charm. "Do you still only date guys who are devastatingly handsome, immensely talented, and filthy rich?"

I bit my lip and cocked my head. "Actually, I thought I'd make a change and start looking for guys who are modest."

The corner of Jag's lip quirked up.

"Besides..." I continued. "I don't really care about all those things."

I don't know what was making me go there with him. Alright —I did know. It was the alcohol. I'd always been a sappy drunk.

"So what matters to you now?" Jag prodded gently. "My information is outdated. What's it take to win you over?"

And in the moment I paused to take a breath—to surrender to the notion that I'd go ahead and say it—the first of the songs I'd put in the jukebox came on. *The Caterpillar* was my favorite love song by The Cure—even before Jag had once let it slip when we were in college that he sometimes listened to it when he missed me.

"Not much," I said finally. "When it's the right person, you can have fun anywhere, doing anything."

I was shy all of a sudden—of his intense look and the way he studied my face. It prompted me to look around the bar. Googie's was kind of a dive—dark and with a huge barrel of peanuts next to the jukebox and a well-availed tradition of throwing the shells on the floor.

When I couldn't not look at him anymore, I turned to him and asked the same question. "How about you?" The room spun a little then. "What does it take for a girl to impress Jag Monroe? And to win his precious heart?"

For days thereafter, I would remember the gruffness in his voice when he spoke his answer and how dark his eyes looked in the light.

"A lot."

16 LET ME LOVE YOU

I used to believe
we were burning' on the edge of something'
    beautiful,
something' beautiful.
Selling a dream,
smoke and mirrors keep us waiting' on a miracle,
on a miracle.
-D.J. Snake (Featuring Justin Bieber),
Let Me Love You

JAGGER (ONE YEAR **After That**)

"It's not too late for strippers," Declan leaned over and said from next to me on the covered fly bridge, with a completely serious look. I surveyed the water that surrounded us on all sides.

"I don't think there's an island full of strippers hiding in the middle of the Gulf of Mexico," I reasoned.

Declan rolled his eyes. "What century are you living in?

There are apps for this sort of thing. We tell them where the house is...what time we'll be back, and they just show up." Declan held up his cell phone and waved it a little in his hand. "And, look—we're still within range."

Uh, no.

"When Gunther said he wanted to spend a weekend fishing with his boys, that wasn't a euphemism for something else. How about we save the strippers for *your* bachelor party instead?"

I slid my eyes to Gunther, who sat next to his brother twenty feet away. Gunther and I had settled the matter months before. When I'd stepped right in to my best man duties and offered to throw him a party, establishing that there wouldn't be scantily-clad entertainment had taken all of ten seconds.

"We're not doing strippers, are we?" I'd asked, suspecting I already knew the answer.

"Not the kind of party, son," he'd replied.

And that had been it. From there, I'd taken his theme sugges-tion and surveyed his buddies who lived down south about what might be an ideal fishing getaway. And so it had happened that ten of us were headed out on a boat, awake and drinking at this ungodly hour. I'd rented a sick mansion on South Padre Island for the long weekend. Apart from not getting too seasick, my goal was to make sure Gunther had a great time.

"Well, at least let's order some edibles," Declan insisted. "Annika doesn't let me do shit," he said under his breath, then began thumbing through his phone, presumably in search of a different kind of delivery service.

"You're not in Oaksterdam anymore, Dorothy." I smirked. "Are you sure it's even legal down here?"

Declan ignored me, then yelled over the sound of the motor to no one in particular, "Yo, who brought the party favors?"

"I got you covered, brother," came a muffled voice from the other side of the fly bridge—Gunther's friend from Shreveport who I'd met the night before. He raised the hand holding his beer in a mini-toast to Declan and smiled conspiratorially. "It's real good shit, too."

Declan dropped the hand that he was using to thumb through his phone and gave me a, "See? That's what I'm talking about," kind of look.

He leaned forward a little in his seat. "Oh yeah? Whaddaya got? Maui Wowie? Purple Kush?"

Gunther's friend frowned briefly and waved his hand in dismissal. "Not that shit..." Then a slow smile came over his face. "We got a case of General Custer."

The guy on his left side hit him with a hard pat on the back. His friend next to him gave him a congratulatory bro handshake.

"What's General Custer?" I asked.

"The most authentic Civil War-era-style moonshine you'll ever find," Mr. Shreveport's brother piped up.

"A hundred dollars a mason jar is what it is..." Gunther trailed off, rolling his eyes a little at his friends.

"Only the best for you, brother," Mr. Shreveport replied, tipping his beer bottle toward Gunther and raising it again in silent toast. Declan looked back over at me and pinned me with an "Are you serious?" kind of look.

"I'm sorry. Have you met Gunther?" I snarked after the guys on the other side of the boat returned to their own conversations. "You know he lives for this. His friends brought enough alcohol to survive the second uprising of the south."

"I can't believe this shit," Declan mumbled.

"Let him have his geeky fun. It's his bachelor party," I pointed out.

"True," Declan conceded. "It's not like he's gonna be doing this too often once he's married."

Now it was my turn to give Declan an incredulous look. "Come on, man. Their wedding is just an excuse for Zoë to throw a party and buy an expensive dress. Those two have been married since their first date."

Declan said nothing, but seemed, somehow, to brood. I pulled newly-acquired trivia out of my pocket. "Feeling the seven-year itch?" I asked.

I'd recently seen the classic film while out on a date. A year in L.A. had taught me that, for someone building a career around film scores, my knowledge of movies was lacking. You had zero cred in that town unless you knew everything about the movies, inside-out. I'd made the mistake of mentioning to a studio head that I'd never seen *The Shawshank Redemption*. I was pretty sure I'd personally insulted the man.

"Eight years next month," Declan said without much joy. The way he said it made me sit up a little.

"You and Annika doing all right?"

Declan shrugged and didn't answer, which was guy vernacular for, "No, but I don't want to talk about it. When he looked out at the horizon and took another long gulp of his beer, I didn't push. If he wanted to talk, he'd talk.

"We're not like you guys," he said finally.

"Who guys?" I wanted to know.

"Zoë and Gunther. You and Roxy. That special something you have. We don't have that kind of glue."

The mere mention of me and Roxy and a special something poked at that place inside me that I didn't like to think about. But this wasn't about me. Deck and Annika had always seemed tight, in that adversarial, hate-love kind of way. He was lovably unrefined and she kept him in line the way only a woman with four brothers could.

"She gets off on being bossy. You get off on being bossed. There's no law that says you have to be as saccharine as Zoë and Gunther," I pointed out.

But Declan just shook his head again.

"There's this way you move together...this way you *are* together..." Declan cut himself short, as if searching for the words. "I don't know why, but it matters more now.

"And I never hear the end of it..." There was a bitter edge to Declan's voice. "How Gunther sends Zoë Boba tea at work when she's having a bad day...how he had that oil portrait made for her of Lady Antebellum wearing a period dress..."

I just blinked at him for a second. Lady Antebellum was Zoë's toy poodle.

"Dude. What the fuck are you talking about?"

"You're just as bad," he accused. "I heard all about the writing room you had built for Roxy; and how you found the one delicatessen in Paris that made matzo ball soup and had it delivered to her hotel room when she was sick; and for *seven goddamned years* I've been hearing about how you wrote Roxy that song. I'm an Architect for Pete's sake. What does Annika want? For me to build her the Taj Mahal?"

"Annika told you about Paris?" I wasn't surprised that Annika had gotten wind that I'd converted the useless spare bedroom in my New York apartment into an office that was ideal for Roxy. It had custom gray stained-wood shelves laid into the walls with the shelf heights on the bottom the exact size of LPs. On one side was a minimalist writing desk on a fun patterned throw rug. On the other side was a leather bean bag chair on a shag rug next to a listening station. I'd waited until Roxy went on a long trip and had it all done by the time she got back.

But if Annika knew about chicken soup in Paris, did that mean Roxy talked about me? And what did Deck mean, Annika had talked about Roxy's song for "seven goddamned years"? Was it Annika who had a long memory or did Roxy talk about it, too?

"Annika tells me about everything you and Gunther do for Roxy and Zoë that I don't do for her. Ever since all our friends started getting married, she wants us to be this perfect couple. She's like a bridezilla already and we're not even engaged."

Declan let out a long breath through pursed lips as he cast his gaze down toward the deck and shook his head.

"Because she's waiting for you to propose, you dumbass." Yeah. Roxy talked too. "And why haven't you, by the way? The two of you have been together forever. That's probably why she's getting crazy. You've seen how it goes. Half the weddings I get invited to, the couple's only been together for, like, two years."

Declan swung his gaze back over, a glint of hardness still in his eyes. "You're missing the point." His bass voice sounded even lower.

"Which is?"

"That the more she compares us to other couples, the more obvious it is she's not in the relationship she really wants." Declan hid it well, but I saw his pain. "We'll never finish each other's sentences, or have the same thought at the same time. I never even know what to get her for her birthday. And, you know what? I can't even blame her for wanting what you have."

But what Roxy and I had was a mess of bad luck and longing. Loving her had doomed every other relationship I'd ever tried to have. And I resented Declan idealizing the tangled web I'd woven with Roxy in any way. No one knew the toll it had taken on me to be able to hold her but not kiss her; to sleep next to her but keep my hands off; to tell her how much I loved her—it had never gone away—my impulse to tell her every single time we talked.

"Then you're an idiot for believing anyone would want to have a soul-deep connection with someone, then *not* be with that person," I replied a little testily. "Roxy and I have been apart for three times longer than we were ever together at this point."

Deck rolled his eyes at me, then brought the bottle back toward his lips to have another drink of his beer. "Annika's not the only one waiting," he muttered under his breath, just before he tipped it back.

I quelled the urge to punish his smart-assery, because what if it was true? I'd always hoped that if we found ourselves in the same city again, and if both of us were single, and that if our careers weren't totally crazy, she'd give us a chance. But that was a lot of "ifs" and something happened that I'd never banked on: we were fucking phenomenal as plain old best friends.

But could Roxy really be waiting? Letting what happened, happen was one thing, but...waiting? It didn't seem like she was. She'd always done better than me when it came to us moving on. Roxy dated for real. I'd hadn't been in a proper relationship since high school.

"Just don't dick her around," I warned, wanting to admonish Declan in some way and *not* wanting to discuss my predicament over Roxy. Annika and I didn't talk often anymore, but we had a connection that had nothing to do with our clique. We'd had some deep talks when we'd volunteered with one another in the NICU and I cared about her.

"I don't want to string her along." When Declan swung his gaze back to me, there was only regret in his eyes. "I know I can't be halfway in. But if I can't, neither can you."

When he quieted again, I felt sorry for us both. I looked back out to the gulf. Declan was right—I was halfway in. What good did it do me to be with Roxy in mind and in spirit but not in body or practice? And why the fuck was I waiting for everything to align?

"It's complicated," I repeated, as if by rote. It was the same thing I'd said to everyone who I'd ever told my sad story. "The logistics of not living in the same place—"

"—are an excuse," Declan cut me off. "Dude. You can afford your own jet. Most people in long-distance relationships get by with a lot less..."

I fought back a maelstrom of emotion. When Declan put it like that, it did sound kind of dumb.

"She's not always single," I pointed out in a last-ditch attempt to defend my inaction.

"So wait until she is. Jag, no one understands why you and Roxy aren't together. I know what's really stopping me from taking the next step in *my* relationship—not the bullshit reason—the *real* reason. But can you really say the same?"

It was the best question I'd never asked myself, even though I pined for Roxy every day. The shitty part of all of it was, I didn't.

It niggled at me for the rest of the weekend—the notion that it wasn't circumstance. That I had, somehow, gotten in my own way. By the end of the weekend, I reached a shocking conclusion: Declan and I had the same problem. Neither of us knew whether we were what our women wanted anymore.

17 LOVE'S RECOVERY

Meanwhile, our friends we thought were so
   together
left each other one by one along the road of fairer
   weather.
And we sit here in our storm and drink a toast
to the slim chance of love's recovery.
-Indigo Girls, Love's Recovery

ROXY

"My petticoats itch," I groused loudly enough for only Jagger
to hear.

I was suffering a late September day in the deep south—
which meant it felt like the dead of summer anywhere else—in an
elaborate, tight-fitting period frock. Keeping scratchy material off
of my legs, the hem of my dress off of the grass, and shoe heels
from digging into soil was no small feat—especially not when one

hand was curled around Jagger's bicep. But I hadn't seen Jagger in what felt like ages, and I had no intention of letting go.

"Shall I hold your parasol?" he asked smoothly, even managing a straight face, though I could hear the humor in his voice. The groomsmen had gotten away with military-themed suits that didn't look the least bit uncomfortable. He was enjoying this entirely too much.

"Maybe you'd better, before I use it as a bludgeoning device to kill Zoë..." I threatened darkly, placing the accessory in his hand so I could tend more thoroughly to my skirts. Ever the gentleman, he made sure the whole of its canopy shielded me from the blazing sun.

I'd tried to talk Zoë down from her plantation-style nuptials— theme weddings are always a bad idea. Unsurprisingly, she'd resisted, so here we were at one of Gunther's relatives' ancestral homes. I'd thought the get-ups Zoë had chosen for the wedding party would cause us to stick out like sore thumbs, but as I could see from some of the other guests' wardrobes, their friends were pretty into it, too.

I'd handle Zoë later, would let her have her day and all that business. Given my own dating record, I likely had years to find the "maid of honor dress of revenge". In the meantime, I had bigger fish to fry—Declan and Annika had suffered a vicious breakup weeks before, and Jagger and I were running interference. Twenty feet ahead of us, Annika and Declan ignored each other as we made the long trek to the gazebo on the far lawn.

We'd managed to switch things up for the processional— made it so Jagger walked with Annika and I with Declan, but the photo shoot would prove more difficult. Zoë's ten bridesmaids each wore different colored dresses and the trim on each grooms-man's uniform had been customized to coordinate to the dress of his partner.

"Closer, please!" the photographer was shouting, making wide squeezing motions with his hands, the universal gesture for instructing large groups to bunch together until everyone fit in the shot.

"Hands off!" Annika hissed rather loudly at Declan, distracting me from my enjoyment of how good Jagger smelled despite the punishing heat.

I looked nervously at Jagger, then at Zoë—who, thankfully, was too wrapped up in gazing adoringly at Gunther to notice. Still, Jagger took a step toward Annika, pretending to fix her hair before discreetly whispering something in her ear. I watched in awe as Annika's grimace melted into a subtle smile.

"What'd you tell her?" I whispered discreetly to Jagger through smiling teeth as the photographer clicked away.

"You really don't want to know."

Two hours later, I'd delivered my toast, kept scheduled events on track, and pretty much fulfilled my duties as Maid of Honor. The party was in full swing, but on auto-pilot, so I figured it was safe to hit the bar.

"Getting soused before battle?" I asked, sliding up to where Jagger and Declan stood, still looking every bit the part of Civil War soldiers. "Don't get so drunk you forget how to use your bayonets."

Jagger rolled his eyes and poured me a shot from a bottle of Patrón. Declan didn't wait before slinging his own shot back. I eyed the c-note in the bartender's tip jar and saw that a third of the bottle was gone. I briefly considered trying to stop Declan from getting totally wasted, but I got the sense that Jagger was handling him and, fuck it, I needed a drink.

Jagger tucked me under his arm, and the three of us stayed there, talking and drinking. It was like old times except Declan couldn't keep his eyes from lifting every few minutes to check on Annika.

"Are you riding back to the airport with us tomorrow morning?", I made the mistake of asking at some point.

"I was 'til *Scarlett* over there cancelled my fucking flight."

A few heads turned. He'd said it more than a little too loud.

"Time for a walk," Jagger said, grabbing Declan by the shoulder, already pulling him away from the bar. Declan looked back at me, his voice no longer slurred and his gaze momentarily and frighteningly sharp.

"You two did it right...It was better to stay just friends."

I tried to ignore the pang I felt as I passed the bartender back his bottle of Patrón.

Later, while Jagger and I danced and I shamelessly sniffed the aroma wafting from beneath his elaborate lapels, my eyes wandered to a swaying Zoë and Gunther.

"They look so happy, don't they?"

I hadn't realized I had been caught until Jagger's voice broke me from my trance. I didn't—*couldn't*—answer. I was afraid that the longing to have what they had would register in my voice.

That could've been us.

I squeezed my eyes shut, willing my thoughts away.

"Do you think we made the right decision?" he whispered.

So he'd caught what Declan had said. I opened my eyes and found our friend's slumped form, too wasted to move, but still drunkenly watching his ex.

"Hard to know..." I murmured. "A romantic would say we could've been Gunther and Zoë. But if we'd stayed together...we could've been Declan and Annika."

"Promise me we'll never be like that—" Jagger commanded softly, slowing our dancing to a halt, "...so angry that we can't even remember the friendship...so jaded that we can't even remember the love."

"We'll never be like that, Jag," I vowed and he pulled me close to dance again. "Besides," I said trying to keep the sadness out of my voice, "...it doesn't happen like that for most people. The epic romance? It works great in fairy tales but not so much in real life."

I knew I sounded defeatist. I wasn't, normally, but seeing Jagger, plus the wedding, and the breakup had me doing a lot of thinking. And the tequila wasn't exactly helping my filter.

"Most people hope for something like that, but it usually happens that you just meet somebody one day and fall in love." My verbal diarrhea just continued. "I'm actually surprised someone hasn't snatched you up already."

For weeks afterward, I would imagine whether I'd really heard, or just imagined, him whisper softly, "I'm not."

18   CHAINED TO THE RHYTHM

Are we tone deaf?
Keep sweeping' it under the mat.
Thought we could do better than that.
I hope we can.
So comfortable, we're living' in a bubble, bubble.
So comfortable, we cannot see the trouble,
    trouble.
-Katy Perry, Chained to the Rhythm

JAGGER

What are you doing this weekend?

The text sat in the composition window of my phone, written and unsent for the past twenty minutes. Ready to send along with it was a screen shot from her Instagram feed—the one in which she'd just announced that she'd turned her manuscript in to her editor.

She'd been working almost nonstop on the project for the past three months—the authorized biography of a British cult band from the 8os—one that had gained renewed attention after three mega-huge acts had sampled some of its songs. Roxy loved writing about bands like that—unsung recording heroes who had served as influences to other bands. She'd been working crazy hours, but she seemed in her element. I loved that she loved it, but she'd been traveling and I'd missed her.

Her going back and forth to London would have been tough either way—from L.A., the time difference was eight hours. But the urgency with which I needed to see her made it excruciating. Gunther's wedding had pushed me to Code Red. Roxy's dance floor commentary had sounded alarm bells and shown me how badly I had failed. She'd done the one thing I'd told her not to: forgotten.

All in, I chided myself as I kept sitting and still not pressing send. It reminded me of Gunther's bachelor party, which, in and of itself, had kicked me into Code Orange. My plan after that had been to do recon and foreshadow my intentions at the wedding itself. Not only had babysitting Declan turned out to be the ultimate cock block—now I had to dispel whatever anti-happily-ever-after cynicism Annika and Declan's breakup had taught her.

Sleeping.

Roxy's reply to my question came back right away—you know, after I'd quit being too chicken to press "send"

Come to L.A. We've got beds...and sunshine.

Yeah. I wasn't above using the weather as bait. I had more pictures in my back pocket. I'd snagged it from one of those apps that gave snide forecasts about the weather. I'd pulled up the ones for tomorrow in New York and L.A. The L.A. One said, "The sun is shining like a diamond in a goat's ass." The New York one said, "Grab your fur coat, pimp. Holy shit, you're gonna freeze". I sent them hot on the heels of my earlier text and was pleased when she texted back immediately with three emojis that were laughing their asses off.

Unless you have other plans?

I'd become a master at fishing expeditions. I'd thrown out countless hooks over the years to ascertain her every status.

California seriously sounds great, but I'm warning you...I'm really, really tired.

I didn't want to sound desperate but I was done with being ambiguous. Like Declan said, no more half.

So we keep it low-key. No wild nights. Besides, I really want to catch up. I miss you, Rox.

The fifty-four seconds that it took her to answer felt ten times longer than that. Because short of her coming here or me going there, I didn't have a Plan B. I might have held my breath as the gray dots that indicated she was typing bounced across the screen.

I'm in. Gimme a minute. I'll go in now and book a flight.

———

TWENTY-FOUR HOURS LATER, Roxy was, indeed, sleeping. Only, not in her apartment—in my house. As I lay next to her in far more clothes than I usually wore to bed, I ran back over my plan.

Declan's push back had taught me something: there was no one big reason why we'd never gotten together—no one big Dragon to slay. I had to look at all of the smaller reasons and eliminate them one-by-one. The list was shorter than I'd made it out to be, and each one was medium-sized. My goal for now wasn't to tell her how I felt—it was to triage where each of us was.

Step one was to find out her relationship status. For years, we'd operated on a need-to-know basis. My guess was, I only heard about a guy if she'd been dating him for a while. We'd never told each other about casual flings, or braided each other's hair while we talked about our crushes. Unless she volunteered something, I would have to ask.

I was trying to avoid that outcome, because I'd be fishing for other intel. If I fished for too much, too soon, things would start to get weird. Number two on the list was finding out the status of her job. She'd done a solid two years with Carson, and was doing plenty of solo gigs. She was rolling along, but I didn't know her plan.

Number three was finding out whether she'd changed her mind about where she wanted to settle. New York had grown on her, but she was still lukewarm. And with all the time she'd been spending on the road, what if she'd fallen in love with a new city? There was no denying that the music industry was basically New York, Nashville, and L.A. Still, I needed to know which way she was leaning.

And the hardest one was number four: did she still have strong enough feelings for me? Or had I fooled myself into thinking I was more than an old flame? All these years, I'd hoped that our chemistry would trump all else. But I'd had to face a hard fact: most days, what I wished was true, unwavering faith was little more than bravado. The part of me that was terrified I'd lost her warred with the part of me that believed in the indelible nature of true love.

"I'm such a shitty house guest," her sleepy voice murmured from next to me. "I told you I'd be a drag."

"You're perfect," I came back with a tiny smile, figuring if I wanted out of the friend zone, I'd better double up on my double entendres.

"How long did I sleep?" She yawned and pushed up on both elbows, covering her mouth as she scanned for a clock.

"Long enough that every place in the neighborhood is already serving lunch."

She blinked, still a bit bleary-eyed, then sank back down onto her back and turned to smoosh her face back into the pillow.

"God, your bed is so comfortable."

You can stay as long as you want.

It had been nearly six months since I'd closed on the spacious bungalow in Marina del Rey. It was one Roxy had seen with me during an earlier trip. I'd been in the market for a new rental— something large enough to accommodate my piano. The place next door was the one up for rental—when we arrived we found out it was taken; I was ready to get back into the car to go see the next place, but since I liked the area, Roxy insisted we check out the one with the 'For Sale' sign.

I'd be lying if I said I didn't take it because she loved it. Her eyes lit up with something I had never seen as we walked through the bright, spacious rooms. It had two large and two medium sized bedrooms which, for me, would translate into a master, a guest room, a recording studio, and an office. Its proudest features were an exceptionally sized backyard, particularly for California, and floor-to-ceiling windows in every ocean-facing room. The master bedroom had a fantastic private deck with a fire pit and a Jacuzzi, and fantastic ocean views.

"This is a great place, Jagger," she'd said. "Plenty of room for your pianos...and so inspiring."

I didn't miss the wistfulness in her voice.

"If I bought it, you could come here and write," I suggested. "... when the New York winter gets too cold, or, you know...whenever you wanted."

"So let's order in again," I suggested, bringing my thoughts back to the present.

She'd arrived the previous evening. We'd ordered Thai and eaten on the deck that overlooked the beach. She'd told me everything about the band whose book she'd just finished—about visiting their home towns and their old haunts in England. I'd told her everything about the film I was working on and our vision for the score.

Still, it felt like a segue—like asking questions about what was next would feel like an extension of the previous night's conversation. We ordered In 'n Out Burger from Door Dash and lounged in bed with me awake and Roxy snoozing until the food came. When I came back in from paying the driver, Roxy was setting up plates in the same spot we'd eaten the night before, except her gaze was caught on something down below.

"You got a hammock?"

The freestanding piece of furniture sat on the lowest tier of my terraced backyard, halfway between the back door of my house and the actual beach. The upper terraces held a dining table that seated eight, a circle of Adirondack chairs and a fire pit, and a Jacuzzi. It also had some pretty serious landscaping, that involved trees, bushes and masonry that added both beauty and privacy. It would have been too dark for her to see much of it the night before.

"I like hammocks." I set the bag and our two shakes down on my glass table. "If memory serves correctly, you do, too."

The truth was, I'd always fantasized about the two of us, as a couple, lying in it. I hadn't climbed into any hammock without thinking about Roxy since I was seventeen.

"Wow, just...a hammock on the beach?" She stood there fixated for another few seconds, now with a hand on her hip. "Okay. I admit it. I'm jealous."

"We could install one in the guest room in New York...have a sand pit put in..." I pretended to muse.

She gave me a look that said "you just would, wouldn't you?"

"Or..." I continued, eager to plant yet another seed of what I hoped would be our future. "You could move to California, and all of this and more could be yours..."

I spread my arms open like a game show host, as if motioning to things on a stage. When she hip-checked me and went back to setting the table, I reached into the bags and pulled out a fry.

Only after she'd uttered an "Oh God, I miss In 'n Out Burger," after her first swallow of her Double-Double Animal Style, did she resume non-foodgasm conversation, though her comment was unexpected.

"I think it's time I grew up."

"What's that mean?" I raised my eyebrows as I squeezed the contents of tiny ketchup packets on to my plate.

"I dunno—have my shit a little more together. Kind of like you, I guess. Get my own place. Go for some of the more competitive jobs now that I've got a few chops. Cash in on all those dues I've paid."

Where's she going with this?

"In New York?" I tried to sound casual.

"Probably not." She'd paused on eating her burger, and looked out at the horizon, which meant she had something on her mind. "One of the projects I'm considering would bring me out here more. It would help me decide whether I might want to move back out west..."

I didn't even attempt to hide my smile, or the words that spilled from my mouth after that. "You know you miss it," I claimed boldly. "You can take the girl out of L.A., but you can't take the L.A. out of the girl."

Her face flushed, and when she spoke, there was a funny quality to her voice. "Funny...I was thinking the same thing."

"So take it," I practically demanded. "Take the job."

...at which point I will fully implement my plan to woo you and win you back once and for all. No high school shit and no more fucking around. I'm bringing out the big guns.

"Seriously, Rox—" I said instead. "We'll hang out all the time. We'll see shows. I'll introduce you to all my friends. You can find a place in Marina Del Rey..."

Or, you could live with me, right here.

"It's still just a "what if." I'm in the running, but they haven't contracted me for the gig yet."

She took another bite of burger and my mind raced to the possibilities.

"What about you?"

I smirked. "When am I gonna grow up?"

She rolled her eyes. "After this movie wraps...are you gonna stay in L.A.?"

I thought of how to word my answer. I didn't want to signal that I would rule out any possibility that would involve being with her. With a shrug, I settled on the simplest of statements.

"I'm open."

She raised an eyebrow. "Open to what?"

"Like you said...I'm ready to cash in on some of those dues I paid and finally do something for myself."

Roxy looked suspicious. Rightfully so—I was being vague. But talking in code was what we did. I didn't want to scare the hell out of her, so I had to drop the breadcrumbs one-at-a-time.

"Anything specific?" she wanted to know.

I put down my burger and wiped my hands. "All the things that come next, after you've got the career and the house and the car."

As she studied my face, I knew she was trying again to decode my words.

"So you're open..." she trailed off.

I thought again of how to say it without spooking her.

"I'm done sitting at home wishing for the things I'm too scared to go after. If I'm ready, I need to put myself out there, for real."

"And what happens if nothing comes of it?" She knew what I was talking about by then. I saw it in her widened eyes, but I couldn't tell whether my insinuations filled her with hope or pity.

"If nothing comes, then nothing comes. But at least I've got to try."

19 BEFORE YOU WALK OUT OF
MY LIFE

I made the choice when you couldn't decide.
I made the choice; I was wrong you were right.
Deep down inside I apologize.
Never meant to cause you no pain.
I just wanna go back to being the same.
Well, I only wanna make things right
Before you walk out of my life.
**-Monica, Before You Walk Out of
My Life**

ROXY (SIX WEEKS **Later)**

1 missed call

I blinked at the alert message that road blocked me on the
lock screen of my phone. I hadn't even heard the thing ring, even
though it had been sitting next to my bed all night. Thumbing in
my code, I navigated to my text app and saw that the call was

from Jagger. Even stranger: he was one of only four people in my life whose calls could cut through my Do Not Disturb, which meant that if he called, I should have at least heard it ring.

The other two people who could get through to me were my dad and Carson, but it was rare for either of them to call. My dad had been schooled and Carson knew the score instinctively: I needed mental space—in the form of peace and quiet—to crank out words.

But I only kept my Do Not Disturb on during working hours anyway—the setting was on a timer. And Jag and I had an understanding about acceptable hours to call. He kept it to before midnight on the east coast if he just wanted to shoot the shit. The call I'd missed from him had come in at two o'clock in the morning.

Shit.

It was with a growing sense of dread that I dialed into my voicemail. I might have called him directly, but what if something horrible had emerged? It wasn't pleasant to think about, but shit happened. Parents died. If it was anything like that, I wanted to prepare. Better that I get myself together than to force him to process my shock.

But the most shocking thing was an emergency itself. Neither of us ever initiated calls that late. But the message he left offered no satisfaction. If anything, it only set me more on edge.

"Roxy." Jag sounded out of breath—not *in danger* out of breath. More like euphoric, and maybe a little drunk. "Sorry if this wakes you up—I know it's the middle of the night there, but..." he trailed off and continued to catch his breath. "But something amazing just happened. And you and I need to talk. In person, love. We need to talk in person."

We need to talk in person.

Never in the nearly-seven years since we'd lived in separate cities had Jag made such a request. If he had something to tell me, he told me. If he wanted to hang out, we made plans. Summoning one another for urgent audiences wasn't something we did.

Now it was I who was out of breath, and not in a pleasant, euphoric way. Jagger had never been so cryptic—or sounded so frantic—and I was scared.

"I know it's short notice," his rambling message continued. "But could you come to L.A.?" I could picture him running his fingers through his hair as he continued. "I met someone, someone who's changed everything."

His message continued, but my mind stuck on his words. My stomach dropped at the words I'd always dreaded to hear.

Oh, God, I said to myself, even as I tried to focus on the rest of his message.

"Something's happened, and I need your blessing..." Please— if you can—just get on a plane."

But he must have reached the message limit length, because it cut off after that. Fifteen minutes later, I was still sitting up in bed, staring at my phone. I'd listened to the message three times more, my sense of dread growing with every new pass. And, now, I wasn't just out of breath—I was shaking.

Something amazing just happened.

I met someone.

I need your blessing.

We need to talk in person.

It terrified me given the thing he'd said the last time I was in L.A.

I want everything that comes after.

I need to put myself out there, for real.

I'm open.

I was sick with comprehension of the one thing this had to be. I finally got my fingers to work and navigated to the right number.

I couldn't call him back, not yet, but my other best friend picked up on the first ring.

"Zoë," I sobbed, "Jag met someone. And I think he wants to propose."

PART 3
TRUE

20   WHAT'S UP?

Twenty-five years and my life is still
Trying to get up that great big hill of hope
For a destination
I realized quickly when I knew I should
That the world was made up of this brotherhood
    of man
For whatever that means
-4 Non Blondes, What's Up?

Zoë

"Jagger's getting married?" I repeated loudly, throwing Gunther a questioning look. "Since when?" I wanted to know.

As he looked up from the morning paper, my husband looked as baffled as me. He shook his head as he placed his coffee mug back on the table and pointed at my phone.

"Roxy?" he mouthed. I nodded.

"Since *yesterday!*" Roxy sobbed miserably from the other end of the phone.

"To who?" I wanted to know. Gunther and I were the kind of couple who told each other everything. That meant, if Jagger were serious with anyone, was thinking of proposing, or had even asked Gunther's advice for how to buy a ring, it was information that I would already know.

"I don't know," Roxy wailed, then proceeded to ramble off years' worth of regret in my ear, about how she'd been there last month and had missed her chance to tell him then. Five minutes into her one-sided diatribe, she'd sailed straight through self-flagellation. She was now whining about how she'd have to pretend to like Jagger's wife.

"Sweetie..." I soothed, but she just kept rambling. I'd tried to talk her down a few times, but it was clear she was far gone on her own trip. At some point, it seemed wise to just put her on mute and have a side conversation with Gunther.

"He told her he's getting married?" he asked once he saw we were muted. "I talked to him last week. He's not even seeing anybody. I gave him shit for being single."

I frowned a little at Gunther. What was he doing playing Cupid with Jagger? Jagger didn't need to find a girlfriend. We all knew he belonged with Roxy. But I'd deal with my husband later. For the time being, I unmuted the phone.

"Sweetie, are you sure?" I said a little louder this time, trying again to get her to slow down. She finally quieted and I seized the opportunity to say the one thing that might talk sense into her. "He didn't say anything to Gunther, and they talked just last week."

Roxy sniffled loudly, and I heard her blow her nose. Roxy was tough as nails. I could count on one hand the number of times I had witnessed my friend cry. I could hear that she was devastated. I would be too if I thought I'd missed my chance with

Gunther. I couldn't think of anything more tragic than the love of your life finding someone else.

"What exactly did he tell you, Rox? Maybe this is all just one big misunderstanding. Tell me what happened," I implored. "And start from the beginning."

So, she did—she told me about the "something big", and about meeting someone, and about flying to L.A. and telling her he wanted her blessing. He'd never said the words "I'm getting married". But I had to admit—what he did say didn't rule out that possibility at all.

But the rumor could be easily confirmed. One call from Gunther to Jagger, and we'd have the whole story locked down in minutes. At one point, Gunther unpocketed his phone and looked ready to do just that. But I raised my hand to stop him. Because, even if this was a misunderstanding, Roxy being this unhinged was a problem. Her reaction was too strong—her feelings to raw—for her to push them right back under a rock, even if she was wrong and not a word of this was true.

"I thought we were moving toward something..." She was rambling again. "If he's happy, I really do want to support him, I just...I don't know how I'm gonna pull myself together. And I'm, like, *a total disaster*, but his message made it sound like he wants me to get there soon. He told me to come to L.A., like—*now.*"

She sniffled and said nothing for a long minute. I could sense the wheels turning in Roxy's head as she concocted a plan to keep running from her feelings. Knowing Roxy, if Jagger really was getting married to someone else, she'd put on her game face and help him plan the wedding. She and Jagger were the two biggest gluttons for punishment I'd ever met.

"You know you have to tell him, right?" I offered gently, certain she wasn't even considering it.

"Yesterday I knew it," she replied between sniffles. "I even had a plan. After last month, I thought..." she took a shaky breath.

"I don't know what I thought. But now that I know he's found someone else, can I really do that to him?"

My jaw might have actually dropped.

"Before this all happened, you were seriously planning to tell him?" I repeated with incredulity, half out of shock, half saying it out loud for Gunther's benefit.

Gunther abandoned his paper altogether. Both of his eyebrows were now raised.

"I've kind of been shuffling things around on my end," she mumbled. "Making it so that, if I wanted to, I could move to L.A. I told him I was considering a move. I just didn't say the reason why I wanted to move in the first place was because of him."

She sighed dejectedly. Any way you cut this, it was messy.

"Rox, what do you want?"

I already knew the answer.

"I want him to be happy," she said it without a moment's pause.

"Sweetie, what do *you* want?"

This one took her longer to say.

"I just want him."

We were both silent for a long minute. I thought carefully about what I could and couldn't say. There were secrets that weren't mine to tell. And, even if I were at liberty to say how many times Jagger had admitted to Gunther how much he still loved Roxy, they didn't need a matchmaker—they needed to step up on their own.

"You've been pretending for six years, Rox. Do you really want to sign up for another fifty?"

For another long minute, I only heard her ragged breathing from the other end of the phone.

"If I'm off base, or out of line...it'll take away what little of him I have left."

Her angst was palpable, and I knew the stakes—losing Jagger

was her biggest fear. But she'd lose him anyway if this went unsaid between them.

"Either that, or it could give you all that you lost, back."

More silence. More ragged breathing. More palpable doubt.

"You think he still feels that way about me?" A note of hope shined through the fear in her voice.

"You obviously think he could, or else you wouldn't be considering a move to L.A. Did it occur to you that maybe he's settling for someone else because he thinks he can't have you?"

"Do you know something I don't?" she came back quickly, with suspicion. "I'm fucking serious, Zoë—now is *not* the time to hold out on me." Her voice had risen to a panic. "I'm on the verge of a nervous breakdown here. Exactly What are you saying?"

"I'm saying that you know Jagger better than anyone in the world, and if your instincts told you the two of you had a chance, you'd be cheating him by not letting him know that he has options."

"I can't go there and throw myself at him..." she argued weakly, but her voice was losing its fight.

"But you *can* go there and choose to tell him the truth," I concluded. "And, Roxy—it's not against the law to show up looking fabulous."

21 TRUE

I bought a ticket to the world
But now I've come back again
Why do I find it hard to write the next line
Oh I want the truth to be said
-"True" by Spandau Ballet

ROXY

Biting my nails wasn't nearly as fun when they tasted like cellulose varnish. I might have thought of that before spending the morning at the spa. I didn't know how, but Zoë had gotten me into The Peninsula at—literally—a moment's notice. I'd been plucked and pedicured until I was clean and tidy, massaged and facialed until I was relaxed and the puffness was gone from my eyes. My hair had been deep conditioned until it held a frightening shine. By the time I got home to pack my bag, my doorman had deliveries for me from four separate boutiques. And, so I sat on the plane, trying not to lose my luster as I headed to my impending doom.

It had never been lost on me that Jag never introduced me to women he was seeing. He'd never brought anyone he was dating back to Rye. He'd never brought girls he was dating tag along when we hung out together. If Jagger was finally introducing me to a girl, it had to be serious. But Zoe was right: if I thought we had enough of a shot that I'd just cinched a cross-country move, Jagger—more than anyone—had a right to know.

That was the other thing I hadn't had a chance to tell him yet. I'd only found out myself that week: the gig I'd been looking at in L.A. had panned out. Not only that—my on-again, off-again free-lance gigs with Rolling Stone had turned a corner and they'd given me a regular column.

More than anything I'd worked for over these past three years, I'd worked for my own freedom. Because if there was one thing being apart from Jagger had taught me, it was that I never wanted to be stuck. I'd made it a career priority—no, a life priority—to make it so that I could work anywhere I wanted. Because anywhere Jagger was, was where I wanted to be.

But now you waited too long, and you could be too late, a voice in my head mocked. Attempting to ignore it, I thought ahead to what would happen when I got off the plane.

Jag and I had played phone tag all day, and then I'd had to get on my early evening flight. With the time difference, I'd be at LAX at 9:00 PM. He'd meet me at the airport and take me to a late dinner. That's when he'd tell me his news.

I'd been too scared to mention anything about said news, by the way. My only hope was that he didn't bring her. I doubted he would. We each knew some part of us would always be in love with the other. Unless he was out-of-his-mind starry-eyed and lovesick for this woman, he'd break the news to me alone.

I was counting on that. My plan was half-baked at best and I needed it to work. I had the script all worked out in my head.

He'd say the dreaded words: "I met someone, and I think I'm really in love. I want to propose to her, but I want your blessing." He might even ask me to help pick out a ring.

That would be my cue to make my confession: "If you're in love, Jagger," I would say, "...then I'm happy for you and wish you all the best. But, if there is even an iota of doubt in your mind, I want you to know you have options."

See, that there was a problem. The words were accurate, but I couldn't think of the right way to say it. When I said it in my mind, it always came out overly suggestive. I pictured myself covering my hand with his and raising a provocative eyebrow on the word "options". Which was truly disappointing, because I was better than this and should have been capable of a much, much stronger script. I mean, come on...I was a fucking writer.

What the hell is wrong with me? I thought no fewer than thirty-five times on the plane, almost willing time to go faster so I could just get it over with. But, of course, it didn't, giving me more time to come up with absolutely nothing. I was less confident walking off of the plane than I'd been when I'd gotten on.

But, when I laid eyes on Jagger, thoughts of my plan disappeared, and I was lost in the smile I loved so much and sage-colored eyes. And then he was hugging me tightly and breathing my name into my hair. Tears sprung to my eyes, and I held him extra long, to give me time to hold them back.

"You're more and more beautiful every time I see you, love," he said with a kind smile before taking my bag. He put his hand on the small of my back as he ushered us toward the exit. "Sorry to rush, but I'm parked illegally and we have reservations for dinner in Culver City. It's gonna take forever to get across town."

In the car, I stalled; took radio control; ribbed him about his car, a new S5 convertible he hadn't had six weeks ago. Inside, I was kind of freaking out. We were barely twenty-five and Jag had bought a convertible and gone out and found himself a fiancée? Was there such a thing as an early mid-life crisis? If there was, it was clear Jag had been afflicted.

"Any word about the gigs you were looking at out here?" he asked at one point. But I didn't know how much I should tell him. Because if he really had met someone, I needed an out. Then, I remembered Zoë's scolding: Jag couldn't walk through a door he didn't know was open. So I laid it all bare.

"I got the job."

22 TO LOVE YOU MORE

Don't go you know you'll break my heart
She won't love you like I will
I'm the one who'll stay
When she walks away
And you know I'll be standing here still
-Celine Dion, To Love You More

JAGGER

"Are you serious?" I asked, uncaring that we'd just pulled up to the restaurant, and that valets had opened both our doors. I couldn't think of a single thing better than Roxy moving to L.A.

"Is this city big enough for the both of us?" She said it jokingly, but there was something behind her words.

I wanted to come back with a lighthearted comment. "For you, I'll make room," I would have said, but there was something weird going on with her.

"Come on, love," I said instead. "Let's go inside and talk."

I would find out what was going on with her before the night was over, but I was bursting with my news. All day, I'd obsessed over how to tell her and now I just needed to get it out. Wanting to be polite before diving into a heady topic, I decided to wait until we'd ordered drinks and appetizers to bring it up.

I was blabbing about how this had been an "it"-spot back in the sixties when the Rat Pack had hung out here. My voice was more nervous than I liked when I regaled Roxy with trivia about celebrity scandals that had earned it notoriety in years since. Before I could finish recounting a rumor involving Sheryl Crow, Trent Reznor, and a little too much to drink, she interrupted me with evident trepidation.

"Just tell me."

My knee-jerk response was to feign innocence, and I didn't know why. Instead I grimaced. Why was I getting so worked up to tell her?

"Jagger...why am I here?"

All these years later, there were only a handful of things of which we never spoke aloud. For the first time in years, I was going to bring up one of them. I liked to think the things we spoke of least were the things we treasured most: we never talked about her song, or about all the times we'd almost kissed, or stolen moments on a summer night in Spain.

"I have something to tell you, but I don't know how you'll take it." I admitted this with sheepish apprehension.

"What are you afraid I'll say?" She frowned a little bit.

The anxiety-slash-elation I'd been feeling all day rose higher in my chest. "I'm afraid you won't approve."

"And if I don't?" she challenged lightly.

I answered honestly. "If you don't, I'll pull the plug."

"Just like that?" She cocked her head.

"Just like that," I said in earnest.

She thought about this for a moment. I didn't know what she was getting at, but, then again, neither did she.

"Don't take this the wrong way, okay?" she hedged. I nodded, and she continued. "Why does my approval mean so much to you? I mean, whatever this is, you said you'd walk away from it. For me. But, whatever it is, it's obviously important."

Nothing's more important to me than you, I thought.

What I said was, "Your friendship is worth more."

She looked anguished as she shook her head. "Than your happiness? Jagger, it's a lot of pressure to have this much power over you. What if you ask me and I give the wrong answer?"

Now I was getting worried. Now it was my turn to frown.

"There is no wrong answer, Rox. Someone wants something from me but it isn't mine to give. If she wants to have it, she has to get it from you."

The strangest look crossed her features then: confusion; hope; disappointment. I didn't understand it.

"What if I'm too selfish to give it up?" she asked.

I realized two things in that moment: for one, we weren't talking in hypotheticals. I was also fairly certain she didn't know I was talking about her song.

"You don't have to give up anything," I said quietly, scolding myself not to hope I was right about her code. Because what would have prompted her to come here and talk about that?

I studied her face unabashedly, too worried about what the hell she was talking about not to look for clues, but too chicken shit to ask the question I'd never been able to bring myself to ask.

"What is it that you don't want to give up?" I asked finally, not wanting to push. Whatever was going on with her, I didn't want to back her into a corner. Roxy looked just about like she was going to cry. It seemed like she kind of already was when she huffed out an anguished laugh that came out more like a sob. She gave me the saddest look I'd ever seen from her then, with knitted brow and shaking head.

"Something I'm not even sure is mine."

Holy fuck...

Our waitress passed by our table. I was too frozen to move. My heart was in my throat and my gaze was still locked with Roxy's. When my body remembered how to move again, I thrust a shaking hand in my pocket and reached into my wallet for some bills. My hand was still trembling when I rose and extended my hand to Roxy.

"We're not gonna do this here."

––––––––––

ROXY

"Wait." Jag was halfway to pulling me up, but I resisted his pull.

"If I don't say this now..." I trailed off. I could hear my heartbeat pounding in my ears. "I'm terrified," I admitted in a whisper.

It was then that he pushed in next to me, having already come over to my side of the booth. I think we were both trembling when he took my hands.

"Don't be," he breathed back, the fear that had been in his eyes just moments before suddenly replaced with an encouraging glint. And there he was—Jag my cheerleader—cheering me even into my doom.

"Remember how we talked about me moving to L.A.?" I began. "It's not because I miss the sunshine. It's because I want to give it a try—with you."

My teeth clamped down on my bottom lip as I watched Jagger blink in surprise, as I watched something tender—possibly pity—come over his face. But I couldn't stop. I had to go on.

"The thing is, I'm not scared anymore. I got what I wanted all those years ago—Brown was what I wanted for myself and Juilliard was what I wanted for you."

"Roxy—" his ragged voice came, springing tears to my eyes. I squeezed his hand to stop him from his talking.

"I swear I'm not doing this out of fear, or spite, or even jealousy. I was going to ask you, over Christmas, whether it was something you wanted, too. But since I heard your message this morning, I'm terrified that it's not."

His warm hand came to cup my jaw, his thumb sweeping under my eye, wiping away my tears. His eyes were full of a tenderness I could hardly bear.

"So, I'm sorry. You weren't supposed to find out this way. I never wanted to back you into a corner. But I can't let you ask me for my blessing on something like this without you knowing where I really stand."

However strong my desire to close my eyes, to shield myself from his reaction, I fixed him with my gaze. It was the most important and heartfelt of confessions and I needed him to see how much my words meant. But watching him, steeling myself for his reaction—whatever it may be—was the hardest thing I'd ever done. Whatever came, I deserved it. It was me who'd walked away.

"It's big enough for the both of us," he said gruffly. I had no idea what he meant.

"Los Angeles," he explained, determination seeping into his voice. "It's the perfect size for you and me."

I shook my head to clear the fog. I didn't understand.

"I'm sorry, too, Roxy..." His eyes softened even more. "I think my message may have left you with the wrong impression."

23 HEAVEN

Oh thinkin' about all our younger years
There was only you and me
We were young and wild and free
Now nothin' can take you away from me
We've been down that road before
But that's over now
You keep me comin' back for more
-Bryan Adams, Heaven

JAGGER

Roxy was shaking like a leaf. I didn't mean to upset her further, but it still felt wrong to do this here. I held her hand every second that I wasn't shifting gears during the twenty minutes it took me to drive us to my house.

It was hard to fathom what she had just told me at the restaurant—difficult to accept that we'd each had the same plan. Pulling my car into my garage, I cut the engine and hastened to get out myself so I could go around and open her door.

"Let me show you," I implored.

She looked as confused as she had at the restaurant, but I extended my hand. It dawned on me, as I noticed how her eyes scanned for details as I led her toward the office, that she was looking for evidence of a woman. How could she not know that she was the only woman for me?

"We're here," I said as I flipped the light on in the small room that served as my office. It was also a recording studio. One long wall held a desk and all my computer equipment, while the opposite one held a deep bank of desks with sound boards of all kinds. Through the window above the sound mixing equipment was the room where I played my piano. And, it really was my piano—the same Steinway that I'd played for countless hours honing my craft.

I sat her down on the wheeled stool that stood before the sound boards while I searched my desk for a shallow stack of papers. When I found them, I sat down on my own desk chair and reached forward to roll her forward so she and her chair were much closer, seated loosely between my legs.

"Read it," I commanded gently, shoving the papers toward her.

She shot me a nervous look before taking them, as if placing them in her hands would cause her to burst into flames. But she did take them, flipping over the front cover, which simply held a memorandum addressing the item to a Mr. Jagger Monroe from a Ms. Barbara Gerrard of Warner Brothers Studio. I watched Roxy's face carefully for recognition of the name—being in the business, I thought she might have heard of her.

She read aloud.

This Confidential Disclosure Agreement is entered into effective May 1st, 2019 ("Effective Date") between Warner Brothers

Studio ("Studio") and musical composer Jagger Monroe ("Composer") having a principal place of business at 1401 Joshua Lane, Marina Del Rey, CA.

Whereas the Studio wishes to conduct activities relating to the musical direction of an optioned film ("Project"); and

Whereas the Composer is the originator of the musical piece entitled 'Destinata'; and

Whereas a third party, Ms. Roxanne Vega ("Owner") is the owner of the musical piece entitled 'Destinata',

The Owner hereby licenses the usage of the musical piece 'Destinata' for the optioned Project and the Composer agrees to arrange additional renditions for the film

She stopped reading aloud, her lips mouthing the words too quickly for the sound to escape. When she glanced back up, she looked gob smacked.

"They want to buy your song?"

"It's your song, Roxy. It always has been."

"But, how?" she choked. "I thought...you stopped playing it for me. I thought you hadn't played it in years."

"My sound editor heard it by mistake—he was looking for a different song file on my hard drive. He said it would be perfect for a different project he was working on. When I told him it wasn't for sale, he thought I was just too nervous to put anything out there. He essentially stole the recording and submitted it to a producer at Warner Brothers."

I studied her face, for any reaction, any indication of what she was thinking.

"They loved it, Roxy," I whispered. "They want it—bad. I got a call out of the blue for a meeting, so of course I took it. They took me to dinner last night. They thought I was just playing hardball when I kept saying no. They offered me more and more money, but I finally told them I had written the song for you and wasn't at liberty to sell it. So they found out who you were and wrote you into the contract. The revision was on my doorstep before I even got home."

Her breath was rapid as she looked back and forth between me and the contract. I could tell it was taking a little while to sink in.

"That's when I called you—late last night after I got home. I figured I'd better stop blocking this and let you decide whether you want to sell," I prattled on, her silence making me nervous.

"S-so the amazing thing that happened..." she stuttered in question.

"...was getting offered a spot for one of my compositions on a major movie score."

"And the person you met..." she continued.

"...was a record executive." I cringed.

"And you wanted my blessing to sell your song."

"*Your* song," I corrected again gently.

"And you needed to see me in person so I would sign the contract?"

"No," I said firmly, "I needed you to come because I didn't think it was the sort of thing to decide on the phone. In retrospect, I suppose I could have come to New York but I thought you might want to meet with Warner Brothers yourself and, I admit, I was a little drunk."

And this was the moment I'd been anticipating, the moment when I learned whether my song still meant anything to her. It helped to know that she still wanted to be with me, but *Destinata* was something we never discussed. How many times had I played that song when I wanted to feel close to her, no matter how many miles we were apart? I'd made a recording of it once— did she still have it? Did she ever listen to it?

"So, there's no one else?" she asked, looking broken. "No girl-friend, no fiancé?"

I tucked her hair behind her ear before cupping her jaws in my palm and leaning in to brush my lips across her soft ones.

"My Roxy...how could you forget what I told you not to? It's always, only, ever been you."

———

ROXY

The kiss that followed Jagger's confession was of the epic variety, the kind belonging to a type of romance I had mocked just months before at Zoë's wedding. It was desperate, yet sweet. Slow, yet frenzied, hands caressing and urgent, yet fusing us together. When we came up for breath, I was on his lap, straddling him across his chair, leaning my forehead to his.

"I love you...I love you so much," he breathed, a long tear sliding down his face.

It was all a dream, him standing us up, sweeping me bridal-style into his arms. I closed my eyes and rested my head on his shoulder as he carried me to his bed. He placed me down, and began undressing me so gently, so intimately, I sighed at his feather touch. He left a trail of delicate kisses on the places where he'd just removed clothing, divesting me of all but my bra and panties. His eyes roved my nearly naked body, longingly, but only for a fleeting moment, before he dug into a drawer and recovered one of his old t-shirts, which he pulled over my head.

I climbed back a bit on his bed, taking in the view as he unbuttoned his jeans, pushed them down to reveal tanned, muscular legs. Jagger was just as lean as before, but thicker. Right down to his snug-fitting gray undershirt and his green striped boxers, grown-up Jagger was ten kinds of sexy.

I yawned, prompting Jagger to look at the clock. When my eyes followed, I saw it was past midnight, which meant it was past 3:00 AM in New York. Between the emotional stress of the day and the late hour, I was exhausted.

"Tonight, we sleep," he said, pre-empting me from finding my second wind. "Tomorrow morning, we do everything else," he murmured a bit cheekily as he helped me into bed. I wasted no time stealing another long, delicious kiss before burrowing more deeply into his embrace. Just before I felt myself drift off completely, I heard him whisper to me, "Welcome home."

EPILOGUE

> In a couple of years they have built
> a home sweet home,
> with a couple of kids running in the yard
> of Desmond and Molly Jones.
> **The Beatles, *Ob-La-Di, Ob-La-Da***

ROXY

"Danzig?"

"No."

"Deftones?"

"No."

"Death Cab?"

I looked up at Jagger and rolled my eyes. Maybe agreeing to consider a rock band for our son's middle name hadn't been such a great idea. I was 37 weeks pregnant, so we really needed to get serious.

"Divo?"

"It has to be a band we *like*," I intoned. "Besides, I don't know why you're giving me bands that start with 'D'. I already told you ten times—our son's name doesn't need to spell out an acronym, like yours."

The stupid delight that Jag had gotten all his life from his initials spelling out the word JAM was one of many new things I'd learned about him since we'd reunited. He'd wanted to pass down his middle name—Anderson—to our little son. Thinking about all of this far too hard, he'd reasoned that if our son's first middle name started with a "D", our baby's initials would concatenate to ADAM.

Jagger looked up at me with truly pathetic puppy dog eyes.

"Pleeeeeease?" he asked sweetly. "I'll rub your feet again."

Hmmmm, tempting...but I had to remain strong.

"Give it up, Monroe." I commanded, sticking my feet out for him to rub anyway. (He did.)

Never in my life would I forget the day we'd told Jack and Elsie our good news. In their retirement, they had bought a place in Santa Barbara where they could come for the winter. That put them roughly forty-five minutes away from our house in Marina Del Rey, where I'd moved into with Jagger the previous summer. We'd only done the long distance thing for ten weeks, but it had still felt like ten weeks too long. We'd seen each other often, during that time. I made it so that the book project I was working on at the time took me to L.A. more and more. Even without that, there were other meetings to attend to every few weeks since we'd jointly decided to license my song.

And so our courtship had commenced—when I came, Jagger took me out on dates. He was as sweet as I'd ever seen him. I'd have been content to watch paint dry, as long as we were together, but Jagger was set on making up for lost time. We discovered our own L.A., together, while turning his house into our home, bit by bit.

But half the time we spent in the bungalow was on the bed. And half the time out of the bed was spent bent over the back of the couch, against the wall of the shower, splayed out on top of his baby grand.

In that department, Jagger was even more talented than I'd remembered, though over the years I'd often wondered whether I had only built him up as the best lover I'd ever had in my mind. It was no figment of my imagination—only he had ever found that special rhythm; only he knew the right way to do me slow, and hard, and deep. Then there were the other skills, skills I didn't want to think about how he'd learned but that served me very, very well.

"T and T, Roxy?" Elsie had asked that day as she'd walked me to their spacious backyard. On these Sunday visits, it was customary for us to have drinks before dinner at the large covered table by the pool. Jagger and Jack usually tossed back a sixer of beer before moving on to the scotch while Elsie and I sipped away at Tanqueray and tonics, and talked. The Beatles-only rule had endured the years, and made everything feel like home, even with the new digs.

"No thanks," I had hedged lightly. "But I'll take a soda. Do you have any ginger ale?"

She'd stopped mid-gait, stepping back from me as her eyes flew to my midsection, then up to my eyes. The bathing suit cover-up I wore was loose and flowy, but still she could tell...

"Oh, Roxy!" tears had sprung to her eyes. "Are you expecting?"

I smiled, not needing to say the words for Elsie to hear the answer. Her joy was palpable, and my hormones were working overtime, so before I knew it, we were hugging, and both in tears.

"Looks like the cat's out of the bag," Jag had said when he found us on the patio, seeming not at all upset that we'd agreed to wait to tell them together. Ever since Jagger had heard the news, he'd been bursting to tell everyone—it was I who'd wanted to wait.

"What cat?" Jack had asked as he stepped in behind Jagger, handing his son a beer.

Jagger collected me into his arms, my back to his front and set a gentle hand on my little bump.

"Dad, Roxy and I are pregnant."

Jack had beamed. "Son, that's fantastic!" And soon he had kissed me on the cheek, shaken Jagger's hand and pulled a teary-eyed Elsie into his arms. Five minutes later, I was sipping my ginger ale from a champagne flute while the other three drank the real stuff. The tone changed from elation to something more somber, but hopeful, when we told them the rest.

"We'd like to call him Anthony...if that's alright with you."

I had put my hand over Elsie's as I asked permission, looking between she and Jack. It had been my idea; one I'd said straight-away to Jagger as soon as we found out we were having a boy. Anthony was the name of their son who had passed away when he was a tiny baby. His little brother was the reason why Jag had volunteered for all those years in the NICU.

"We'd be honored," Jack had replied with gruffness in his voice.

Soon after, we'd sat for dinner, where I ate twice my normal helping. By contrast, Elsie was too excited to eat. By the end of the meal, they were all drunk (having opened a second bottle of champagne), laughing and singing along to *Ob-La-Di, Ob-La-Da*.

"How about David?" Jagger asked, pulling me out of my thoughts and back to the moment. His voice was different when he mentioned this one—less joking than it had been a minute before. "David, like, as in, Dave Grohl."

I smiled at the memory.

"He did sing us our first song," I mused, remembering our first date at The Vermillion Room.

"Anthony David Anderson Monroe," Jagger said smiling hopefully. "I think it sounds kind of nice."

The truth was, I did too. In my mind, I ceded my earlier position before he even pulled all hundred and seventy pounds of me into his loving arms.

"ADAM it is," I said, grinning at the irony.

Anthony kicked spiritedly, as if approving our decision. Jagger clicked through the iPod until he found *Ob-La-Di, Ob-La-Da*. I giggled as Jagger sang, intermittently to me and my gargantuan belly. My little son finally had a name.

———

Hey, readers—Kilby here! Did you like *Ended?* Check out the bonus materials for Ended on my website (https://www.kilbyblades.com/ended-by-kilby-blades-bonus-materials), including the soundtrack to the book!

If you think I'm funny, and you like a little heat, *The Art of Worship* is my award-winning Romantic Comedy novella about a virginal 18-year-old who turns to his dad for sex advice. It's hilarious and a fan favorite, because sex is awkward. And, when you're a teenage boy, so are man-to-man talks with your dad. This one has mature themes, so be warned.

"*Readers looking for a tale that blends soft-core sex, romance, humor, and feminism will enjoy* **The Art of Worship.**"
- IndieReader (Julia Tilford)

"*This book is tremendous…it has all the sexual tension, creative encounters, and unique story that I wanted. It also had the non-clinical elements: the connection, the learning curve, the different gender perspectives. It was really beautiful.*"
- Go Away, I'm Reading Blog

"A *sex manual disguised as a novel; this should be required reading for every teenage boy.*"
- Ed Morakowski

And—love it or hate it—please, please, please leave a review for *Ended.* For freebies and other awesomeness, join my newsletter, where I overshare about my crazy life (https://www.kilbyblades.com/readersubscribe) and learn about my new releases by following me on BookBub!

ABOUT KILBY BLADES

Kilby Blades is a *USA Today* Bestselling author of Romance and Women's Fiction and a fifty-time award-winning author. Her debut novel, *Snapdragon*, was a HOLT Medallion finalist, a Publisher's Weekly BookLife Prize Semi-Finalist, and an IPPY Award medalist. Kilby was honored with an RSJ Emma Award for Best Debut Author in 2018, and has been lauded by critics for "easing feminism and equality into her novels" (IndieReader) and "writing characters who complement each other like a fine wine does a good meal" (Publisher's Weekly).

When she's not writing, Kilby goes to movie matinees alone, where she eats Chocolate Pocky and buttered popcorn and usually smuggles in not-a-little-bit of red wine. She procrastinates from the difficult process of writing by oversharing on Facebook and Instagram and giving away cool stuff related to her fiction novels to her newsletter subscribers (https://www.kilbyblades.com/readersubscribe).

amazon.com/author/kilbyblades

instagram.com/kilbyblades

goodreads.com/kilbyblades

facebook.com/kilbybladesauthor

twitter.com/kilbyblades

BOOKS BY KILBY BLADES

The Gilded Love Series

(Gilded Love Series Box Set - Coming in 2021)

———

The Hot in the Kitchen Series

Romancing the Stove (Coming in 2021)

The Modern Love Series

Friended eBook | Friended Audiobook

———

Standalone Contemporary Romance

The *Worst Holiday Ever* Anthology Series

Non-Fiction Author Guides

(Coming in 2021)